Performance Art

PERFORMANCE ART

STORIES

DAVID KRANES

UNIVERSITY OF NEVADA PRESS | *Reno & Las Vegas*

University of Nevada Press | Reno, Nevada 89557 USA
www.unpress.nevada.edu

Cover design by Iris Saltus

Some of the stories in this book appeared in earlier form in the following publications:
"The Daredevil's Son" *Fiction* (2010)
"The Stand-Up Phobic" *Spring* (2015)
"A Man Walks into a Bar" *New West* (2012)
"Escape Artist" *Nimrod* (2002)
"Target Practice" *Ploughshares* (2006)
"The Warren Beatty Project" *Esquire* (1991)
"The Weight-Loss Performance Artist" *Isotope* (2008)
"The Photojournalism Project" *Image* (1996)
"The Fish Magician" *Great Basin News* (1997)

LIBRARY OF CONGRESS CATALOGING-IN-PUBLICATION DATA
Names: Kranes, David, author.
Title: Performance art : stories / David Kranes.
Description: Reno ; Las Vegas : University of Nevada Press, [2021] | Summary: "Part of our socialization is the urge-to-perform. We perform images of ourselves for others. If we are successful, we are urged to perform. For some, the urge is so great and the talent sufficient that we become performers. *Performance Art* is a book about performers and performances that are extreme. Most of these stories and their performers and performances are at the edge of dream"—Provided by publisher.
Identifiers: LCCN 2021008819 | ISBN 9781647790141 (paperback) | ISBN 9781647790158 (ebook)
Subjects: LCSH: Entertainers—Fiction. | Performance art—Fiction.
Classification: LCC PS3561.R26 P47 2021 | DDC 813/.54—dc23
LC record available at https://lccn.loc.gov/2021008819

The paper used in this book meets the requirements of American National Standard for Information Sciences—Permanence of Paper for Printed Library Materials, ANSI/NISO Z39.48-1992 (R2002).

FIRST PRINTING

Manufactured in the United States of America

For Carol and for Ron Carlson . . . both of whom have let the show go on and stayed when either the performance or the performer failed

Contents

Performance Art

The Daredevil's Son

Spit 'n' Image

Everyone said Lucas looked like his famous daredevil father. When he was no more than a baby, people were pointing. "He has his father's eyes!" they said. "He has his father's ears, his teeth, his chin." And when Lucas became more active—first reaching, then walking—just like that, people noted his stride and grip. "He's going to be a handful," they'd say. "Will you look at those shoulders! Check the chest!" They dubbed Lucas *the spit 'n' image*. "If that's not the Old Man all over again—call me Oprah Winfrey!"

The Old Man was, of course, Lucas Sr.—the Madman of Motorcycles, the Hysteric of the High Wire, the Lost Lunatic of Wild Lion Prides—a man who had *done it all* and had the medical history to prove it. Under the disfiguration and scar tissue, Lucas Sr. was an anatomical pincushion. He'd given *Death-defying* a new syntax and grammar—leaping the world's major rivers, lowering himself into active volcanoes. He'd put saddles on Lear jets and ridden them from Santa Fe to Cancún, driven a mass-transit bus, in February, down the north face of Mount Rainier. Lucas called *fear* "nerve on sick leave," and bragged he'd never lost an arm wrestle with The Impossible. He was a hard act to follow—never mind follow in the *footsteps of.*

Still, people looked from son to father, father to son, and "Spit 'n' image!" they'd say. "Spit 'n' image!"

The father failed to see the resemblance. "Where're the skin grafts?" he'd say. "Where's the quartz eye?" He called his son *Baby Face*. "Shove Baby Face up against a chain-link or cyclone for a week or so—*then* there'll be a resemblance," he joked. Still, he *liked* the comparisons. He liked imagining scenes, like when perhaps the two of them—Lucas & Lucas, father and son—would, joined at the hip, straddle a burning Kawasaki midair, high over the Grand Canyon or the Snake River. He imagined himself retired and Lucas Jr. breaking the longevity record for hypothermia. *Fearless* steps aside! Behold the *Son of Fearless*.

Dressing Up

Barely five, Lucas Jr. discovered his father's cedar walk-in closet. It was like the mouth of a monster and smelled like teeth and leaves, pine cones and wood. If the house was silent, no one around, Lucas-the-boy would slip in and shut the door. In the dark the closet seemed like a cave straight out of "Ali Baba and the Forty Thieves." On some days the still air was cold, but on others it was as hot as Arizona. Closed in, Lucas Jr. could smell his father when he carried him under his arm, sometimes, through crowds. It was a smell not unlike that of wet and dark scavenger birds. Inside his father's closet, the whole point seemed—for as long as Lucas Jr. dared—to sit in the dark, which was like some kind of hairy and thickening secret, one with muscles and veins and scars, like his father's raw arms.

By the time he was six, Lucas Jr. was trying everything on: goggles, gloves, helmets; then the leather coats and jackets, which hung, like-but-not-like, his mother's dresses—trailing against the hardwood floor. Sometimes he switched the light on to inspect himself in the full mirror. If he stood close, he looked smaller; if he stood further away, he looked like a bad dream of himself.

The point was: his father's skin was everywhere. His father's clothes hung like sheets and sheets of skin—so that, finally, what Lucas Jr. was dressing up in, trying on, wasn't his father's clothes at all—it was his father's *body*. Sometimes Lucas Jr. felt evil dressing up, as if he had no worthwhile power at all. Sometimes he felt more like an angel or god—all radiance and breath. Sometimes he felt that he could fly; his father's jumpsuits had crow feathers sewn into their shoulders and were studded with black-agate crow eyes. Sometimes—there seemed so much hammered and studded weight—he felt as if he might fall and fall, coursing through fire and water and air…forever.

Then—at the age of ten, maybe eleven—he switched to his mother's closet, and discovered that he felt more at home there. And her clothes fit better. In his mother's closet—surrounded by her very dissimilar wardrobe, rich and dark—Lucas Jr. felt far more cherished and possible. He liked the weightlessness of the fabrics. He loved the soft, friendly animal sense of his mother's stoles. He felt himself to be in a space where people brought him food and comfort. He felt—in a single stroke—both on display and free. He felt older. He felt closer to being some kind of worthwhile being, some kind of champion or king, a cartographer of his future. What was happening? Why was that?

When he moved back, briefly, to his father's closet, it seemed that the sleek, sweaty animal and raptor smell of the gloves and leather coats and crow feathers had disappeared. The secret of the dark felt less powerful, the dark itself less dark, the sense of bears hibernating, of stallions copulating, less rank and raw and wintry. What had felt like the larceny of crime-syndicate birds was gone. Now when he growled in his father's closet, he only felt silly. When he raised his arms like wings, he felt shy. But in his mother's closet, when he threw his soon-to-be-broad-boned shoulders back in a kind of triumph, something electric happened in the cave of him and his tears welled up in his eyes.

Vanity…Vanity!

One piece of furniture more than any other whispered to young Lucas. It was in his parents' bedroom, and what it whispered was *Come close!*

Lucas Jr. called the furniture piece *my mother's desk*. It had a flat top with bottles and brushes, tubes and jars. It had drawers down both sides and a mirror behind it, which was shaped like a birdbath or plastic wading pool. Its legs were like the legs of a thin animal, and between them was a rose-colored upholstered bench. Whenever Lucas Jr. obeyed the whispering and came close, his mother's desk would whisper again. *Go ahead*, it would say. *Sit. Relax. Think about yourself. Try things.* His mother's desk gave him permission—he would open tubes and jars, dipping his small hands into creams, feeling fine powder between his thumb and fingers. Sometimes he would shake drops of scent onto his palms and then rub them onto his face. He explored rouge and lipstick. There was a life-all-its-own at his mother's desk, he thought.

When his mother was somewhere else, maybe out shopping, he came close to the desk and took the permission it offered. He would lean forward toward the mirror and try to find his mother in his own face. Was he the spit 'n' image of his mother as well—did people think? It was hard to tell—hard because usually his mother was not in the room where he was but in another. When he tried to evoke her, she was almost always a room away and through a door frame—standing with a cigarette in one hand, its smoke curling around her, and what she called a "highball glass" in the other.

Lucas Jr. could lose time; time could dissipate like his mother's cigarette smoke. And in one of those lost times—on an afternoon when he had wrapped himself in some chiffon and a stole—he suddenly, in the mirror, *saw* his mother, framed by her bedroom door and standing behind him.

She was silent for what seemed a long time and then asked, "What are you doing?"

"I don't know," he said. "Sitting at your desk."

"It's not a desk," she said.

"It's not a desk?"

"It's a vanity."

"A—?"

"Vanity…vanity!"

"Vanity," Lucas Jr. repeated. "Vanity-vanity."

"And where did you get what you have on?"

"Is this a squirrel?" Lucas Jr. asked, lifting the stole. "It feels like a squirrel. Like a squirrel looks."

What Do You Want to Be When You Grow Up?

In the off times between Lucas Sr.'s death-defying tours, the family entertained roadies and wannabes. Men and women in exchangeable jumpsuits and sunglasses began asking Lucas Jr.—when he circulated, offering buffalo wings and guacamole—"What do you want to be when you grow up?" Did he want to wrestle professionally? Did he want to go on *American Idol*? Some of the party people addressed him as *Younger*—a name his father liked to bandy—Hey, Younger! Was Younger going to be a daredevil like his father?

At first the interrogations paralyzed him: *What did he want to be when he grew up?* He had no idea. He hadn't even considered it. But after a while folding and refolding the question was the one thing he looked forward to when he climbed the board-wide stairs to bed.

He liked to swim. He'd watched the Olympics. Sometimes he told the party people, "Michael Phelps." He liked Johnny Depp; he liked Jim Carey. Sometimes he told those who asked, "I want to act; I want to be in the movies." One time when he said that—when he said, "I want to be in the movies"—a blond woman at the party (who'd lit a famous match that had famously incinerated his father) said, "Honey, be careful." He told people that when he grew up he'd like to be on *Nova*. He said he'd like to deliver the mail. Never, though, in all the asking, did he say *daredevil.*

"So then, you don't want to be like...do what your father does?" people asked.

"No, because my father scares people," Lucas Jr. said.

"But hey, Younger, people *like* to be scared," guests responded.

"*I* don't like to be scared," Lucas Jr. said.

"Are you sure?"

"Some people think my father is the devil," Lucas Jr. said.

"But sweetie, to be the devil and be paid for it!" a woman said. The other guests around her laughed.

"Be the devil?" Lucas Jr. queried.

Parents' Day

When Lucas Jr. was in the sixth grade at J. Carter Middle School, his class had a Parents' Day in February. Brain-surgeon parents came with models of the hippocampus. Realtor parents came with lease agreements and PowerPoints about gated communities. Lawyer parents came with personal-injury slideshows. Then Lucas Sr. came and dove off the school's roof into sixteen inches of water in a plastic pool.

"Are you ever scared?" a classmate asked Lucas Sr. at the class gathering afterward.

"Fear!" Lucas Sr. began, then paused. He calibrated the checked-breathing among the twelve-year-olds. "Fear...is a cripple on downers," he said.

Members of the class looked at one another in puzzlement.

"What he means is..." their teacher, Miss Forbes, began. But then she couldn't finish her sentence.

"So what did they think?" Lucas Sr. asked Lucas Jr. that evening over tacos and chile verde.

"They were amazed," Lucas Jr. said.

"*They were amazed!*" Lucas Sr. repeated. "As well they should be! I'm in the Amazement Business!" And he hoisted his Dos Equis in the direction of Lucas Jr.'s mother and chortled.

Advanced Placement

Lucas Jr. grew. You could almost see him doing it; day to day, it was like time-lapse photography. By the time he was fifteen, he stood six foot seven and weighed almost three hundred pounds. Now in high school, he took courses in the automotive arts and in calculus; he took advanced metal shop and Chinese. His guidance counselors worried that he lacked focus. He played goalie for the school's hockey team and filled the net. Girls were frightened of him. *Boys* were frightened of him. He was frightened of *himself*—though he couldn't understand precisely why. "Something bad's going to happen to me," he confided to his mother.

"It's called a growth spurt," his mother said.

He tried talking to his father in Mandarin.

His father told him, "Save it for the Ming Garden."

Lucas Sr. bought a skateboard, a snowboard, a Kawasaki. He took the Kawasaki apart and put it back together again.

"It's about time we started training," Lucas Sr. said.

"It's still hockey season," Lucas Jr. responded.

"What's this thing you've got with hockey?" his father asked.

"I like the pucks flying at my head," Lucas Jr. said. "I like the slap and penalty shots. I like the mask."

"I'll get you a mask and you can wear it when we jump the Rogue River—or when I set you on fire," his father said.

"It's not the same," Lucas Jr. said.

"I'll get you a Chinese mask. You can pretend you're doing Chinese opera when you go off the ramp."

Imagine a Net

On his son's sixteenth birthday, Lucas Sr. brought Lucas Jr. to the roof of their house, where he'd bolted down a four-foot-diameter trampoline. Theirs was a peaked roof, which created a raked trampoline. Lucas Sr. had covered the roof of the garage—fifty feet away—with foam rubber and rags.

"I call this Guided Imagery," the father told the son.

"I don't understand," Lucas Jr. said.

"You imagine a net," Lucas Sr. said.

"I imagine a net?"

"You imagine a net that—if you miss the garage roof—will catch you."

"What do you mean: *If I miss the garage roof?*"

Lucas Sr. explained about the trampoline and the trajectory. "I imagine a net."

Lucas Sr. explained how it was going to work. He would have Lucas Jr. close his eyes, then see the number 10 in his head...then see the number 9...then 8. And so on. After the number 1, he would then imagine a zero. "'Let it get larger,' I'll be saying to you. 'Then larger.' Then when it's larger than you are, you walk through it. When you're all the way, when you're through it, then you imagine a net strung between the house and the garage. It will come. And when it comes, you'll understand how you can be immortal. And then," Lucas Sr. explained, "then you step up and onto the trampoline and begin to generate your momentum. I'll be on the garage. I'll have gone first—shown you how. Then—when I say 'Go!'—you go. I'll be there to guide you. Once you do it—once you sit on the air of the world like a hawk or blackbird—you'll be a member for life."

Suddenly Lucas Jr. became aware of his mother standing below them in the driveway—small and tucked into herself, looking like a corncob. "Please!" she was barely saying. "Please...please, Lucas, please. Younger...don't."

"Imagine a net!" His father shouted at him.

"I imagine a net," Lucas Jr. said, meekly and uncertainly.

"Please," he heard the husk figure of his mother repeating below.

"The rest is mystery," Lucas Sr. announced.

And so it was. But was it air or light or silence that the boy, Younger, found himself catapulted through late that afternoon?

Early Decisions

Senior year was confusing: he was a *junior*—yet he was a *senior.* His counselors advised him: Go for early decisions. So Lucas Jr. applied. He applied to MIT and Julliard. He applied to Scripps and the Art Institute of Chicago. He applied to the University of New Mexico and the University of South Dakota. He solicited recommendations, wrote entrance essays, brought financial-aid forms home to his parents.

Lucas Sr. was silent on the subject for nearly a month before he asked, "So what's this college shit?"

"Honey—" his wife—holding a single tentative hand up—cautioned.

"The boy—" Lucas Sr. stopped himself, took a breath, nodded for a beat of five, then continued, "the boy doesn't need college."

"College broadens," Lucas Jr.'s mother tried.

"The boy can create a website. The boy can speak Chinese. The boy can paint a boot you'd all but try to put on. The boy knows how to make a pipe bomb. He can inoculate mice. He's written country and western songs that have been sung—okay, just one of them, but still—in Nashville. What are you talking about, *broadens*? College *broadens*?"

Lucas Jr. asked for another helping of short ribs.

"So what's all this college shit?" his father repeated.

"People should have options," Lucas Jr. tried.

"People should have—excuse me—what?" Lucas Sr. pressed him.

"Options," Lucas Jr. said.

"Options." Lucas Sr. rolled the word around his mouth, as if it were a piece of gristle from one of the evening's short ribs.

Think about Being Invisible

On the eve of Lucas Jr.'s graduation from high school, his father presented him with an alligator jumpsuit—insisting that, right then and there, he try it on.

Lucas Jr. swam in it. "It's too big," he protested.

"All the better to grow into," Lucas Sr. beamed. He took Lucas Jr. by the hand. "Something else I want to show you."

The father drew the son—hand in hand still—out of their house and down the drive to the family's stand-alone three-car garage, where—using a coded remote—he rolled the aluminum door of the middle bay up. Inside, under the white light of the fluorescents, Lucas Jr. could see that his father had repainted his touring bus. On the outside—in blood-red Rockwell Extra-Bold font and ringed by acrylic flames—was printed: LUCAS & LUCAS/A GREAT TRADITION OF DAREDEVILS!

"So what do you think?!" Lucas Sr. asked. Grabbing a bottle of Herradura tequila from his workbench, he uncorked it and took a hit. He passed the bottle to his son. "Fabulous—right?!" he said and then encouraged his son, "Go ahead. Drink."

Lucas Jr. lifted the bottle with a flourish in the same way his father had, drank—and choked.

Lucas Sr. did a drumroll on his son's back to quiet the coughing, and when Lucas Jr. finally had his breath back, asked again, "So—c'mon; tell me—what do you think?"

"I think—" Lucas Jr. began, then stopped, his throat still raw and dry and burning. And then he said what he thought and felt: namely, that he had mixed feelings about being a daredevil.

"Hey: it isn't an option," his father said. He took the tequila bottle back and slugged from it. "Not an option. You just need to get started. You just need to get... *underway*. Once you're started and *underway*—you'll see; you can't stop."

"Except I'm not sure I want to start," Lucas Jr. said.

There was a silence—as flat and stark as old aluminum siding. It filled the large garage.

Lucas Sr. began to nod—thrusts of his head that became more and more aggressive, like punches. "Son, you either start—and start tomorrow—or you're invisible to me," Lucas Sr. announced. "You either start—or you're a vacant lot. You either start—or you're what's left over after a hurricane. Debris." He took the remote and rolled the middle bay door down and then up again. Then down, then up. He started to chug the tequila. "Think about it," he said. "Think about being invisible. Think about being an orphan."

At Sea

Lucas Jr. chose Deep Springs College in Nevada and dropped out within a month. He lived in a tent at the edge of Zion Canyon and dreamed about parachutes. The wind outside his tent carried a scent somewhere between piñon and tequila. He left and tried a vision quest in the Mojave, where he was found at dawn, sunblind and staggering, by two hiking lesbian epidemiologists named Geneva and Grace and brought to a hospital emergency room in Barstow.

"You're badly dehydrated," the ER resident on duty pronounced.

"Nothing came to me," Lucas Jr. said woefully.

"Those two ladies came to you, and they saved your life," the resident corrected.

"Watch your language," the lesbian named Geneva warned.

"Call me Ross," the ER resident invited.

"I can't be my father," Lucas Jr. said.

"It's a trick—isn't it?" Ross said. "A trick and an affliction that we all need to learn to manage."

"His eyes were almost black," the lesbian named Grace said.

"His tongue *was* black," the resident named Ross said.

"Imagine a net," Lucas Jr. said, and he started laughing hysterically.

He spent two days in the small hospital's ICU wing. "You were very badly burned," he was told. He said that his father knew how to be burned—worse than *badly*; he knew how to be burned and live. "It's a special knowledge," he was told.

When he was released, he thought of going back to school. Did his parents know he was no longer there? It seemed not, because each month more money appeared in his checking account. Maybe, he thought, it was possible; maybe he could imagine a new…or old… maybe he could be his father—or the reflection of his father. Or the shadow. Or the aftertaste.

He bought a Kawasaki and rode it east on I-15 into Las Vegas. He'd seen the documentary about his father leaping the fountains at Caesar's Palace, diving off Paris's Eiffel Tower, swimming naked in the Shark Reef at Mandalay Bay, riding a burning hang glider from the roof of Steve Wynn's Encore.

He tried to reconstruct the smell of leather from his father's closet. He tried to imagine his father's scarves, hanging like sloughed-off skin. He'd seen a Gila monster during his vision quest in the Mojave. He'd seen a diamondback. Both had slithered away. Neither had offered him their poison.

He took a room at the Mirage and swam in their pool, fell asleep in his chaise, and dreamed, again and again, of the ocean. He was at sea in his dream. And then somewhere else—somewhere not-sea—and then at sea again. And then not at sea. And then at sea. When he woke up, a beautiful black woman in a net bathing suit, floating nearby on a polyurethane sea monster, was staring at him. "You've been somewhere, haven't you?" she asked.

The Oldest Profession

Lucas Jr. and the woman in the net bathing suit had dinner at Boucheron, across the Strip at the Venetian. The black woman in the net bathing suit had changed into a summer dress that was more straps than anything else. She cut her lobster ravioli into smaller and smaller pieces.

"What does that mean," she asked, "when you keep saying that you feel helplessly at sea?"

"I keep dreaming of parachutes and the ocean. I can't imagine a net," Lucas Jr. said.

"Are there fishermen?" the woman changed out of the net bathing suit asked. "Are there paragliders? Are there pelicans?"

"There are abandoned scuba tanks—and there's no gravity," Lucas Jr. said.

"Sounds sort of like my condo," the black woman changed out of the net bathing suit said.

Suddenly, on the large flat-screen at the bar, somebody was leaping the lake at the Bellagio in a stretch limo. "That could be my father," Lucas Jr. said. The entire roof of the stretch limo was on fire.

"So is that who you're *with*? Are you with your father here? Are you together, traveling?"

"You could say that," Lucas Jr. said.

"I just did," the woman changed out of the net bathing suit laughed. "Sins of the fathers!" she said and laughed again. "Now you're talking my language." Her laughter made the beads of her necklace dance.

"What language is that?" Lucas Jr. asked.

""Aramaic," the black woman changed out of the net bathing suit said.

"Can you say, *'This is good ravioli?'?*" Lucas Jr. asked in Mandarin.

The black woman responded in a language with lots of glottal stops and gutturals.

"Aramaic?" Lucas Jr. asked.

"Or close," the black woman said. "Or close enough. The oldest language—for the oldest profession."

"So, what is it that you do?" Lucas Jr. asked.

"I'm a guide," the black woman changed out of the net bathing suit said. "I take people where they want to go. To the Promised Land. I help them lose themselves."

Losing as an Art

During the year when it was in Lucas Sr.'s head that he and his son would be the darlings of Prague and Budapest, he pressed Lucas Jr. to get both a passport and a visa. Waking from losing himself with the netless black woman, Lucas Jr. felt that at last he had a strategy. He would travel from distant place to distant place—losing himself. And when there was finally no self—no Lucas and especially no Jr.—he would return to his native soil, if, in fact, at that point he *had* a native soil. And he would walk serenely in through the front door of his house, where his mother would look like he imagined Ophelia in *Hamlet*. And cry. But his father wouldn't even speak his name. His father would stare through him as if through an imagined net. And he would be free. Free forever and ever, he would no longer feel the burden of being the Daredevil's Son. Instead he would open a restaurant specializing in exotic dim sum.

He had over $7,000 in his checking account. It was possible.

He flew first to Helsinki, where he shaved his head and played the acoustic guitar in a waterfront bar. He lost himself in the music, and when the dawn came his shoes were nowhere in sight. On the following day he went by rail to Copenhagen, where his seventh-floor room at a hotel called the Wilhelmina had a balcony. After dark he could see the lights and sails of moored yachts. If he jumped off the balcony, holding onto the four corners of one of his bedsheets, would the white linen carry him out and into the harbor?

He threw a wine bottle at the wall mirror in his bathroom, hoping to make himself as fissured and cracked, as starkly black and silvery,

silvery white as Hans Holbein's *Dance of Death*—images he had once discovered on display in a public library.

If he'd had a beard, he would have shaved it. If he'd had pounds to spare, he'd have gone on a hunger strike. But what was it, exactly, that a hunger strike struck? Struck at? And wouldn't it mean that he would have to have a hunger to strike from? A base? A passion? A base passion?

Instead he gorged himself at a local restaurant on a specialty casserole of cod and potatoes and artichokes baked in white wine. When he returned to the Wilhelmina, he couldn't remember the number of his room and knocked on all the seventh-floor doors until someone didn't answer. And then he tried his key.

He rented an Opel and drove to Lublin in Poland, where he visited the Majdanek extermination camp. He drove to Kraków, where he walked through the Jewish cemetery—a burial ground where the stone markers had been used to pave streets and then, following the war, returned. In the small acreage and under the immense weight of his yarmulke, he felt as immaterial as the industrial revolution. He was among the souls of a people who had lost everything and, there and ashamed, he understood, finally, that losing, like the work of Hans Holbein, was an art.

There Are Other Holbeins, You Know!

He had Hans Holbein on the brain. Everywhere he went in Kraków he saw skeletons: riding trams, selling flowers, eating alone in restaurants. Skeletons. He went to a club called the Cynamin Café, where he drank too much, then staggered down some crooked streets to another club called the Prozak where, at the bar, he rambled on to a stranger. He rambled in English; he rambled in Mandarin. He rambled about pirates and burn units and invisibility. But mostly he rambled about *The Dance of Death*—Hans Holbein, Hans Holbein, Hans Holbein.

Finally, when the stranger had had as much as he could take, he turned face-on-face to Lucas Jr. and shouted, "*There are other Holbeins, you know! Do you know that?!*"

"Other Holbeins?"

The stranger told Lucas Jr. about Hans Holbein the Younger.

Lucas Jr. wheeled from the Prozak out into the night, where he wove between lanes, crossed parks, and went in and out of wrong hotels—finally finding his own. The next day he took a tram to the Wyspianski Museum, which had several of Hans Holbein the Younger's works on loan and where, for nearly an hour, he stood before a portrait titled *Lady with a Squirrel.*

For all the ways in which the painting confused him, it amazed him. The woman looked to exist in the world with almost unearthly assurance. How could that be? She looked all woman. She looked like a man. She looked healthy and unskeletal and like food—her head wrapped in a quilted something that looked like phyllo dough. She was seated, and on her lap was a chestnut-colored squirrel eating a nut. Just over her shoulder, on a branch and almost whispering in her ear, was an oily-black bird—starling or crow—a bird that appeared to have scales rather than feathers.

On a bronze plaque beneath the painting it said, "Hans Holbein the Younger" and gave a date.

Hans Holbein the Younger.

How could a father be so different from a son?

How could a son be so different from a father?

The Homecoming

He flew home unannounced. When he descended the escalator to baggage claim, there were professionally dressed greeters with name signs meeting arrivals. There was a family with a welcome banner and a dozen black and silver helium balloons. No visible placard, though, said: *Welcome Home, Lucas Jr.* Or even: *Welcome, Younger.*

He took a cab to his house; the cab driver was Syrian and unnervingly polite. He kept saying, "My pleasure" and "My pleasure" and "Yes, sir; my pleasure." He offered tea in a small paper cup: "Please," he said. "Did your business go well?" he asked Lucas Jr., but Lucas Jr. wasn't sure how he should answer. Had his business gone well? What was the answer? "Did it go as well as could be expected?" the perfectly-hair-combed Syrian driver asked.

"Thank you. Yes. I think so," Lucas Jr. said.

When they arrived at his house, Lucas Jr. saw a large Re/Max sign on the front lawn. The sign was red and blue: *For Sale* printed on the inflated logo, an image of a hot-air balloon. He paid the Syrian driver and thanked him.

"My pleasure," the Syrian driver said. He bowed from a seated position.

After the cab pulled away, Lucas Jr. stood on the sidewalk with his bags and studied the house he'd grown up in. He smelled smoke. And then, checking the air, he could see the smoke, rising from somewhere in the backyard. He could see what was probably ash falling through the sunlight.

He hiked to the back—down a drive on the west side and through a cedar gate. Now Lucas Jr. could see the broad back of his father in front of a smoldering, sometimes-flaming pyre. He picked up a broken chair and threw it onto the fire, stirring up sparks and ashes.

In a pile near the fire were many items of clothing and more furniture. The younger Lucas thought he recognized some of the items as his mother's. Among the furniture appeared to be scraps of what he'd once called *my mother's desk.*

Vanity...vanity! he heard the ghost of his mother's voice softly saying. *Vanity...vanity!*

The younger Lucas dropped his bags. The sound of them hitting the ground caused his father to turn around. His eyes were the eyes of a combat soldier in a flashback. Everything he wore was denim, but all the denim was shredded. He looked like he'd been in a barroom brawl with a bear.

"Hey," the younger Lucas said.

The older Lucas spat and snorted. His eyes looked smoke-damaged; his hair looked like a grebe in an oil spill. He seemed a figure in a George Romero film. Everything about him was attempting to compensate for a lack of balance, for confusions. He looked through his son as through a bank of air.

"So, what are you doing? I don't get it. What's happening?" the younger Lucas said.

His father turned back to face the fire. He bent to a pile of clothing, plucked up a navy-blue wool skirt, and threw it onto the fire.

"Where's Mom?" the younger Lucas asked his father's back.

"Left—gone," his father said. He threw the word up and over his shoulder like a scrap for a dog.

"What do you mean?" the son asked, and when his father refused to answer, refused to settle, he asked again: "What do you mean? "Left—gone," the father said—his words sounding discarded. "Left—gone," he said a third time.

"Where?" the younger Lucas asked.

"Who the fuck knows?" his father said.

"Did you have a fight?" the younger Lucas asked.

"I don't fight with women," his father said, then bent and threw a Cuisinart onto the fire, where it ignited in oily flames.

"Did she say anything?" Lucas Jr. asked.

"Yeah; she said: '*I need my life*,'" Lucas Sr. said. He still had his back to his son.

"I've been away, in Copenhagen and Kraków," the younger Lucas said.

"Fuck you," the father said. "Fuck you and the turncoat you rode in on."

"I don't want to ride motorcycles over gorges," Lucas Jr. said.

"Tell me about it," his father said.

"I don't want to lower myself into volcanoes."

"Suck my dick," his father said.

"I don't want to be tied up in anchor chains and dropped into the harbor."

"That's because you're a faggot," his father said. And with that he bent and threw two cashmere sweaters and a night table onto the flames. He crouched, removed his boots, and threw them in as well.

"Do you have any idea why you're doing what you're doing?" Lucas Jr. asked.

"Yeah. I do. Absolutely. I'm doing what I'm doing because I'm doing what I'm doing," Lucas Sr. said. "Because it's what a man does."

"It confuses me," Lucas Jr. said.

"Really? Well, you think you're confused? Try me. Try burning up everything belonging to the one woman who was willing to live with you. Try talking to your son—who doesn't even exist. Try not being able anymore to imagine a net. Then you'll be in the ballpark. Then you'll know what confusion is. Welcome home."

The younger Lucas bent, engaged the grips on his bags, lifted them. "I hoped maybe you would wish me good luck," he said.

"Because I have no idea what's going to happen next. None at all. And I thought maybe you would wish me well."

"Well, I don't wish you well," his father said. "But here's a thought. Maybe it will compensate. Maybe it's my reward for getting my picture in the paper so many times. You have no idea what happens next? Try this. Slip your arms through these sleeves and check the fit. *What happens next*... is the thing that happens just before the thing that happens just after it. And hey, that's okay. Don't thank me. All we are is, you know, father and son. It's a small thing. Still, what happens next is the thing that happens just before the thing that happens just after it. You can pass that on to *your* boy—sometime—if you have one."

"Thanks, Daddy," Lucas Jr. said. "Thanks. I appreciate it." With that his bags were in the air, and he turned and carried them back up the driveway. Above him, flying squirrels—with silhouettes like bats—leapt from branch to branch.

The Stand-Up Phobic

Ethan's hair is an air show and he's sweating. Every performance lately seems a conspiracy-theorist's nightmare. Any room he's booked into is slack-jawed and oversized and swallows him. Like a bad Jonah dream. Like having a three-day booking at the Whale. At the House of Ribs. Yeah! Put your hands together—won't you, please—for our own sackcloth and ashes! Ethan Fallon!

Or…or the room's too small. *How small*? Hey! Where Ethan's booked is *so* small that if you blow your nose the EPA'll be there issuing a citation. It's—seriously—*so* small that the front and back doors are the same. And the threshold mat only says "Wel."

So Mr. Fallon, do you think of what you do more as performing…or as, I don't know, kind of like taking your Tourette's out for the evening?

The room's so small that Ethan's nearest EXIT is him*self*.

And sir, hey—I mean it—I really appreciate the interview.

So then, what-you-call-this—you-and-me-back-and-forth—is…an interview?

I don't know; what else—?

Hey, no else. Seriously: no else. And—I mean it—don't pay attention to me; no one does. Or…how about…what-we're-having-here—back-and-forth, you/me—we call a ring-tailed lemur? Or a mongoose. So: how many—is it veterinaries…or veterinarians? Never mind; call them vegetables. How many vegetables does it take to turn a lemur into a mongoose?

Listen, I'm sorry. I didn't mean to make you—

How many—?!

I don't know.

Guess! Lemur into mongoose.

Three?

Close! Four hundred and seven. Four hundred and six for the change operation, and one to carry the ring.

• • •

It's okay, Ethan thinks—the club, the booking, the interview—it's operable…stage 2 maybe; still, he'll get through. And okay: the crowd's hostile, but not all *that* hostile. There's laughter—true, it's only scattered—but laughter. And laughter—whatever your modifiers—can be infectious. Or fractious. Potentially an ear (kind of), nose, and throat subversion. And subversions…well, maybe not *subversions*; more, maybe, *subdivisions*, could be—in the right light—like gold… some of them, anyway; others are more like garlic.

You were brought up—? Your father owned a restaurant in—?

What do you call someone who's afraid of garlic?

I don't—

Seriously: what's our fear-of-garlic-guy suffering from? What do we call him—and don't say, "A cab."

I don't know.

An alliumphobic! Write that down. Log it. It's important. For me. For the interview. Fear of garlic: alliumphobia. Type that into your… whatever, iPad, or tape it over your eye socket—I don't care. Alliumphobia. Should I spell that?

No; I—

Actually: one—one i. A-l-l-i

So, how long have you been doing this?… Stand-up?

Since my dog died.

Since your dog—?

Frankie.

Frankie?

Yeah. As in "Johnny."

Died?

Yeah.

I'm sorry.

He was my best—probably only—friend. He had no phobias.

But that was—?

When he died, yeah.

When you started doing—?

Stand-up. Yeah. He was twelve. Going on eighty-five.

I'm sorry.

He was like—I'm talking about at the end—he was like a grandfather to me.

I'm sorry.

You have no idea.

• • •

How simple would it be, Ethan wonders, to smuggle an IED into the club? Sure, okay, far-fetched. But...hey, look around; *far-fetched* is where you have to be careful. Because far-fetched is what carries the toxins. Always. This is not a world to entrust your knuckles to. *Or* your fingernails. Maybe *especially* your fingernails. Because you don't have to look far. Or fetched. For someone with a gun permit who's drinking Chopin vodka in a trattoria to...it can be as innocent as wallpaper. As guilty as an anthrax-carrying puma.

"My dog died," Ethan announces to the club audience, inappropriately.

"If I was your dog, *I'd* die," a drunk blurts.

"Frankie," Ethan says—naming his dog.

"Frankie and Johnny," the drunk counters.

"He was my best friend," Ethan offers.

"Ten bucks says he was your *only* friend." The drunk's on a roll. He thinks.

"It's possible," Ethan says lamely.

"How close of a friend *was* he?" Now the drunk thinks *he*'s the comedian.

"He was *so* close...," Ethan begins. He clogs up—salt phlegm. "*So* close..." His ribcage ratchets. "*So* close that the two of us..." He can't finish the sentence.

For a split second, Ethan loses his thread. *Are we in the past or present?* he wonders. *Tense.* He can't remember his respiration—or the opening to the Declaration of Independence. He feels he's forgotten how to breathe. Maybe it's the water on the stage table; maybe it's his lack of vigilance. Or virulence. Could be. Can be. Has it come—his *lack*—from...where? A Dasani bottle or just the tap—tiny sink in his dressing room?

Jesus, he needs to be more vigilant, visual, virtual, virtuous—more *careful*! Without knocking, a rogue word, *any* rogue word, can enter and—with no loyalty whatsoever—become systemic, begin touring the rooms of a person's brain. Furnished *or* unfurnished. Either. Both. Take, for instance, the word *Everglades*—a word less than a hair's breadth away from life and death, Troilus and Cressida—so *many* other nouns and modifiers...specifically: being an anagram, almost—*Everglades*—for the word *reversible*.

Okay; *enough*...*enough*, Ethan thinks. *I need to get rid of my head, out of it—back to the room, the interview.* Still, he has the impulse to shout, shoot the word—*Enough!*—like ammunition, through his dressing-room window, because *enough* is *never enough* when your mind shows up in sackcloth, like a beggar, pleading.

In a place with both mirrors and heating vents, there is sure to be desperation. Specialists measure this. Desperation and fear.

"Yeah, right; let's talk *fear*—okay? Order another beer, and talk *fear*. Let's have an adult one-on-one, heart-to-heart about—" Ethan *marks*, and again, *re-marks* his territory. "Let's have a no-holds-barred tête-á-tête confrontation with terror, spar a round or two with anxiety. Take on dispossession, insurrection, gluten intolerance. Even agyrophobia, which is the fear of streets. Surgency and *in*surgency."

Do other people worry? Ethan wonders. *Worry-worry*, not just warehouse worry, that this country is being taken over? By *under*lings? From the Everglades? Probably it's a crock, or...possibly, an entire pestilence thereof. Still, these things happen. Yet—

Also—if the object, even *objective*, of the hour is facing demons, Ethan's got to confess that he has worries about—no small thing—*sermons*. Sermons make him nervous. *How nervous?* He suffers from homilophobia—fear of homilies—and gets on edge, or just this side thereof, in the presence of guys-in-black—women too—who stand (okay, true: not unlike himself) *elevated*...*up* at one end of a room trying to capture the attention of other people with drinks. Homilophobia. Sermons: fear of.

Even *small* sermons, even sermon*ettes*, can send Ethan into total fight-or-flight mode. Anything pastoral. Or just a simple past-*participle* from a sermon—a *blessed* or *broken*—and he begins to worry that he might...who even knows?!—wake up trapped behind an organ. And

Father—seriously!—Whoever, Pastor YouNameIt, will be standing behind a lectern (podium, pulpit) making him—if it's possible—feel contaminated, smaller. Homilophobia.

• • •

I read somewhere that you don't think you're funny. Is that—?

What I said, I think, is: I'm not... I don't... funny's not what I primarily communicate.

What is it you feel you primarily—?

What I feel I, primarily, communicate is a very, very, dark allegory. That this is never this; rather, it's that—but not that ever in a final sense. More... dread. Terror. Laceration. Involuntary lactation. Immunization.

Except—! I mean, if you don't think you're funny, why do you do stand-up?

Excellent! Good equivocal question.

I mean, people have the expectation, I think, that someone—you know, at the mic, in a comedy club, is there because, for whatever reason, that person—

Hey, I'm not going to argue, except... it's a drug reaction—why I'm here and why I go out, go solo, into a dark room filled with strangers, when there's always the danger, even the probability, of the dark room being infested with voices and the microtherapy of glass—why do I go out... why do I go out into such a place? I mean, it's a drug reaction—totally.

I'm not sure I—

Why does any acrobat stay in the circus? Same reason. Why allow yourself to be injected with Velcade when, inevitably—a week later, a month, six months—you know you're going to encounter the worst thing you can dream of. I'll throw out a word, and it's the word neuropathy! Neuropathy. Never mind: just the specter of neuropathy brings me to my knees. So! I mean: What're your choices? Can you answer that? Or mine?! What are your options? What does a person with coulrophobia do?

Coulro—?

Fear of clowns. Coulrophobia! "How do you escape yourself?" really, is what we're asking. So hey: you sign up; you get on board. Rehearse—to the degree you can—in front of a mirror. Tape yourself—learn whatever. Revisit your dreams. Deepest terrors. Check to see that the stove is not lit. Check again. Unlock the front door; lock it; check the lock. Check the stove again. Take the Red Line…Blue Line. Distrust the whole line construction. Arrive. Tell the manager you're here…you're there. Go to your dressing room. Listen to the voices, measure the tensile strength of the glasses out front. Want to run away but instead are grateful that where you are is not a Chinese restaurant because it's not just coulrophobia that's a problem for you. You have consecotaleophobia as well—fear of chopsticks.

• • •

It's a good thing, Ethan thinks—he's glad—*that there aren't many people tonight*. Because in crowds—truth is, with *any* people, others—he becomes incapacitated. So, right, good, we can do the math; he's incapacitated now. Some enchanted evening, in any crowded room, it happens: *incapacitated*. Incapable. Inescapable. So Ethan's hair's not tended or perhaps even un*in*tended, like an April garden—tendrils and shoots with the intent to bloom…but not sure.

"Fat people really frighten me," Ethan begins again, launches. "They take up so much space. And space is air. And air's life."

He chokes to demonstrate. But then the choking gets away from him, and it seems, maybe, he'll need oxygen.

Some in the crowd are half laughing. Some are texting or checking messages. Or talking about Aurora, Colorado. Or maybe it just sounds like *Aurora, Colorado*—maybe it's *oral sex*. So, what are Ethan's best jokes about assault weapons?

Instead he tries three one-liners about STDs. "You know, the word *lesions* is really a funny word, if you think about it," he says.

Half his audience laughs; the others look pissed off.

Ethan does a golf swing and tries two zingers about Tiger Woods.

Someone yells, "I heard that fucking joke three years ago–and it wasn't funny then!"

There's an unspoken *get-this-asshole-outta-here* subtext in the room.

An idea comes to Ethan, so he tries it: "Hey, I love Tiger—love him, really! So I guess that makes me blond and with an IQ of seventy-five."

Another heckler yells out, "So, what's *your* handicap?"

Ethan likes the word *handicap*. It's easier to work with than *pelagic*. So he zooms in on the heckler—who looks, he thinks, like a spider dressed up as a Wall Street broker. "Right, good—*handicap*," Ethan says. "What's my handicap?"

"So far: fifteen jokes!"

The crowd laughs.

"My handicap is..." Ethan squints, lifts then drops his wire-rims to better focus the heckler. "My handicap is, I'd guess, maybe forty-two, forty-three. One hundred seventy-eight...shoes on. Five ten, eleven. Kenneth Cole suit."

• • •

Ethan scrubs off his makeup and consents to his interviewer walking him to Yum Yum—a Thai restaurant on the West Side. *I'm obsessed with their yum woon sen. And this time of night no one's there.* Ethan neglects to own up to the twelve containers of pad prik king aligned in his small flat's refrigerator—containers he can't eat from for fear of contamination but, nonetheless, can't throw out.

You lost your fiancée in a highway accident?

I'd quibble with the words lost, highway, and accident.

For perhaps a minute, the only sound in the dressing room is that of tissues on skin.

I appreciate this opportunity.

You call it an opportunity?

Well, I just hope it's not an imposition.

But you're all right with inquisition.

The interviewer laughs. Stops laughing. *Mr. Fallon—?*

Ethan burns the wipes he's used to remove his makeup. They crackle in a small cylindrical, metal wastebasket.

So, your parents owned a restaurant?

My father.

Who they called "Charlie."

Chop house.

You ever perform there?

I shopped the vegetables.

You chopped? Like a sous chef?

Like an Apache warrior.

Outside, the night looms and attacks and is viral; the lights, strung the lengths of avenues, flicker—devious and vengeful. A sense of menacing intent ambushes all the stalled traffic. The intersections chime with at least seven levels of evil. Where there are pubs, there's paranoia. What is the word for fear of traffic lights? Find it. Memorize it. Lift it with the same care that you would lift a box of Antique Flow Blue Minton Delft.

Ethan and his interviewer scurry across Cornelia Street. *Scurvy.*

Mr. Fallon—? What? The interviewer scrambles to catch up.

Words come into my head. Shit! I worried about this!

Worried about—?

Him! Them! Ethan points to a man wheeling a grocery cart swollen with flopping trash bags. *It's okay; it'll be okay. Stay ahead of me. Stay between us. Run interference. It's my hobophobia.*

Homophobia?

Hobophobia. Fear of beggars. Street people. I shouldn't walk in the city. Because it all comes out—like a bad joke—especially at night. My hobophobia. My dromophobia.

Drom—?

Fear of crossing streets.

I thought you were mostly funny tonight. Can you remember your first joke?

Tonight?

Well, I was thinking ever.

The wind picks up. Every avenue they cross is more vengeful.

They all laughed when I told them I wanted to be a comedian. Well, they're not laughing now.

Mid-block, briefly, suddenly, it's as though someone's lowered the city's audio. Gravity gives way to an aggrieved, even *aggravated*, sense of applause. Muggers fall to their knees, and there's a breach in the city's thick patina of urbanity. Bloodstains evaporate from tenement stoops. At the immediate intersection, a woman in a gorilla suit grips a bouquet of balloons and rehearses Blue Oyster Cult's "Don't Fear the Reaper."

Sometimes the city is beautiful. Sometimes the city makes me breathless because it's so astonishing. But it never lasts. Long. Still, sometimes I'm glad—glad I'm funny when I'm funny.

They pass a dog tied to a bicycle chained to a parking meter. They pass an old woman sitting on a stoop, making a necklace from clothespins. They pass a Trinidadian girl in a tutu–spinning...spinning. They pass a junked Jag with its doors ajar; inside, a young Jamaican injects himself. They pass a parrot perched on an apartment awning, who—almost yawning—repeats the phrase *Peace be with you* in Arabic: *Wa alaykum assalam, Wa alaykum assalam*. Behind them, the dog they passed barks.

Ethan's hair rises and falls, falls and rises, settling finally like elegant mathematics on his scalp—a field so logical and lucid that it makes a person speak involuntarily.

Oh, dear! Oh, my! Ethan says. And then, out of the blue—or purple or gold—of the moment, he says a name. *Frankie.*

After which, the world—measurably—twists, wishes itself to be different. A different world. One undriven by fear, unactivated by regret. One both purple and gold. Bruised and celebrated. They arrive at the restaurant and so it is! Purple and gold. The neon blinks, embracing Ethan. On and off, off and on, purple and gold. *Yum Yum*, it pulses. *Yum Yum*.

A Man Walks into a Bar

Man walks into a bar—*bistro*, actually, with a bar attached—in Vegas. Call the bar/bistro Nora's and locate it west of the Strip, beyond Decatur, on Flamingo. The man's name is Scott Elias. His dealer co-workers—on the swing shift at the Palms—call him *Scottie*, which he hates. When the *Scottie* issue first came up, after he left his Clark County District art coordinator job, he asked co-workers to please call him *Scott*, but when one said, "Dude, lighten up," he retreated.

So, man walks into a bistro, sits at the bar, and considers ordering a double—Chopin vodka on the rocks—but doesn't. Instead he orders a single and slips a fifty into the bill validator for a *Deuces Wild* run of video poker.

Within minutes, a second man—dressed in Levis, cotton shirt, linen jacket—one of a pair eating nearby, approaches, hesitates, stands there studying Scott. Eventually Scott will go *home*—to a two-bedroom on Rainbow, where he lives with a spinally injured eighteen-year-old named Tory Mendez.

Backstory: When Scott first encountered Tory, three years before, he believed him to be a once-in-a-lifetime experience and had been uncannily right. Tory was traditional and nontraditional—a mother with U.S. citizenship, a father without. He'd served in Juvenile, but when they met Tory was an honors student. His paintings—oils and acrylics—were portraits. Every portrait face was engulfed in fire—marking him a year later as a visionary when he became the sole survivor of a car crash that incinerated both his parents on I-94 near Caliente. Tory then outlasted a coma of forty days, after which he'd been like a Marine with his physical therapy until, with the help of two walking canes, he became almost agile.

No other family available—Tory accepted Scott's invitation to move in and make do as they might. "Think of me as a roommate and not a caretaker," Scott had said. *Roommate, caretaker*, whatever—the two fused. They painted together. Scott walked Tory to his rehab sessions. They cooked together. They did tae kwan do together and then their own version of it, which turned cane fighting into almost a martial art. One time, though, making a move, Tory drew Scott's blood, and then reflexively broke into tears: "Jesus, I'm sorry, man; I'm sorry! But Scott joked and called the two of them blood brothers.

But what should Scott *call* Tory? *Roommate? Foster child? Adopted son?* Better: what should he call himself? *Blackjack dealer? Painter? Onetime arts coordinator?*

Okay, present-tense *story* again: So now the man who's walked up to the bar behind Scott Elias and hesitated checks with the man he's been eating with, who nods and signals *Go for it*. The man standing behind takes a breath and appears to be counting—while our own man, Scott, considers ordering a third very cold Chopin. He's not happy. He's ashamed. For six months he's only painted canvasses of blank canvasses because *c'mon! Wasn't that better than not painting?* Christ, the things we tell ourselves!

The man who's walked up behind Scott steps slightly closer, hesitates, clears his throat, hesitates again, says, "Excuse me," waits, then repeats, "Excuse me."

Scott turns, looks at the man. "Were you—? I'm sorry," he says.

The second man introduces himself: *Harley Davidson—seriously, Harley Davidson*—and says, "Listen, cut to the chase, I suppose, but... my friend and I couldn't help noticing you. We're casting agents and—. Look, I'll just come out and say this: You have a *look*; you're very photo—as they say—*genic*. So is there a chance you're—? Are we not recognizing you? Have you done film work?"

Scott assesses the man. What's going on? Is he just being silly? Has someone set him on a dare?

"Listen, I don't mean to intrude," the man says. "Though I am." He smiles—a smile with the caption *Ironic*. "The point is, I'm in town. Casting a new film for—I suppose you've heard of it—*Dreamworks*." He stops, waits. "So hey, don't leave me hanging here: are you in the industry?"

"I'm a painter," Scott says. "Painter sometimes, educator other times." Then he finishes the list: "Also sometimes a blackjack dealer."

"Excellent! Good for you," Harley Davidson says. "Because, you know, painters are... important. Painters are necessary. Painters are cool. So, would you be willing to—I don't know, maybe tomorrow morning—meet with us for a screen test?"

"Would—?"

"Right."

Because he's working his third drink and considers the encounter unreal, Scott agrees to a time and place. Harley Davidson promises that at 10:00 a.m. promptly there will be a limo driver waiting outside Scott's apartment complex on Rainbow. If he were psychic, Scott would be able to scan paranormal space and foresee what awaited at the end of the limo drive: a private corner, high in the Mandalay Bay Foundation Room, in which a diminutive actress named Tina Glazier and he read a four-and-a-half-page scene essentially about silence. "Why don't you ever talk?" would be Tina Glazier's opening line. And if Scott had his psychic sight straight, he would *then* see the moment, after the third reading of the scene, when the group of gathered executives and agents turned first to one another, then out to Scott—one of them asking: "Okay, so who do we talk to? You have an agent?"

Scott says he doesn't need one; he can read a contract. But Harley Davidson tells him, "No, that's not the way it's done" and signs him—needing only a single cell phone call—with an agent. The agent's name is Amanda, Amanda Kelly Malouf. She's twenty-eight and speaks with a voice such as Scott Elias has never heard, in breathy bunches of words. He'll be needed for three weeks and will be paid $2,500 a day during that time, plus a per diem of $300. If he's needed for a fourth week, both the salary and the per diem double. Can he start tomorrow?

On his way out of Mandalay Bay, a man he's never seen asks, "How's it going, Mr. Elias?" Riding in the back of the limo to his place on Rainbow, he asks the tuxedoed driver to stop briefly at the Palms, where he tells his shift manager, Deke, that he's not sure what his schedule's going to be. It sounds weird, he knows, but he just signed for a movie being shot locally, and the shooting begins early tomorrow. Deke, impressed, says, "Whatever. We can work it out."

Deposited back on Rainbow, he doesn't go into his apartment because—what should he tell Tory about the film? So he drives his Toyota to the Orleans, where he walks up to a bar and orders a double Chopin/rocks. On a three-by-four-inch sketchpad he always carries, he draws two columns, heading one *Tell Tory* and the other *Don't.* When he's done, his *Don't* column's up by three reasons; next to one of them he puts double check marks: *Our relationship might change.*

That night at their apartment, Tory shows Scott a new dance step he's mastered with his canes and then unveils a new painting—a portrait from the chest up of an Anglo who appears to be in his late thirties. He's all face and skin and surrounding him is a white-blue crystal structure—like quartz or ice. "What's that?" Scott asks.

Tory confirms Scott's suspicion: *ice.*

"Because—?"

"Because the man is being frozen out of his life. Because I dreamed it."

"What do you mean, frozen out of his life?"

"I mean *frozen out of his life*. Frozen. Chilled totally out. Gone. No more life."

Scott, in some cave of his brain, tells himself it's best not to ask, but then he does. "Not totally—but somewhat—I think he looks like me."

"That's because, I think, he's you and *not* you," Tory says. He feints right and pokes Scott playfully with his left cane. "That's the way he was, anyway, in the dream. Like you...but not. Like his mouth, his chin—that's you. But when he talked, his voice was different."

"It's good," Scott says.

"I don't think *good, bad*," Tory confesses. "I just think *paint*."

"Stay that way," Scott says. And they laugh—neither sure what they're laughing about. Then: "You know, I think—" Scott starts. He holds his hands, palms flat, up in front of the painting, as if measuring something...or reaching for equilibrium. "What I'm trying to get to has to do with balance," he says. "Like, if you tilted his head to the right—you know, to offset the weight of the ice or quartz or whatever, crystals—on the left, it would be stronger."

"You have this thing about balance." Tory does a little drunken walk. Grins.

"Just a thought," Scott says. And then: "The next week or so, I'm going to have to be out of the apartment early. But I've stocked a bunch of breakfast burritos in the fridge."

The following morning, Scott *is* up early and out of the apartment. A driver picks him up and drives him to the location. Harley Davidson is there. "For the first little while," Harley announces, "I'm going to be your coach." And so he is: he explains the scenes being set up, walks Scott from trailer to trailer, offers coffee, fruit, a bagel.

Scott meets people and tries to remember their names and what they do: Melanie—wardrobe; Peter—hair; Laszlo—makeup. He jots the pairings in his sketchpad, where he also lays out a diagram of labeled rectangles, identifying the locations of various trailers. When Harley's not shepherding him somewhere, he studies his notes. A young woman named Cindy gives him script pages, which she calls *sides*. "Your scene will be shooting around 2:00," she says.

It's actually closer to 3:30 when the scene shoots. The director—whose first name is Leonard and whose last name sounds different every time another person says it—explains what he wants, walks people through the steps. Leonard calls it a *rescue scene*. It's a scene in which Brad Pitt "rescues" Hilary Swank from a bar where she's gone to show him she doesn't need him. Scott's the guy who's been plying her with drinks.

"I want you to come this close to killing each other," Leonard tells Brad Pitt and Scott, "but ultimately, I don't want either one of you to lay a hand on the other." He says he wants the whole scene—all four pages—to come in at under a minute and a half. "It's about physical tension. And I'm stressing the word *tension*," he says. Then he asks Scott, "Your name again?" and when Scott tells him, introduces him to Brad Pitt.

At the end of the second take, Leonard says "Cut!" then "Whoa!" and Scott sees him stride over to where Harley Davidson is looking on to confer. While they're huddled, Scott listens to Brad Pitt and Hilary Swank tease each other and smiles even though he doesn't understand their references. At one point Hilary Swank turns to Scott and says, "You were good in that." Brad Pitt agrees: "A lot of tension, dude." Scott says, "Thanks." They ask about his other work, and he says that actually, he's a painter—painter and teacher. He says it's just a fluke he's there; he walked into a bar two nights ago and *blah-blah-blah*—but he figures, you know, what the hell.

When Leonard and Harley Davidson finish their conference, Harley Davidson—all smiles—finds Scott. "Okay, c'mon. Let's go for a walk," he says. On the walk, Harley tells Scott that Leonard was *blown away* by what he did.

"What did I do?" Scott asks.

"Your emotional charge. What you did with your—it's a *presence* thing," Harley Davidson says. "He literally couldn't believe you hadn't acted before." Then Harley drops the bomb: "Leonard's going to have the whole movie rewritten to enlarge your part," he says. "You've just been promoted to the isosceles."

"I'm sorry: *isosceles?*"

"Film term. It means the third side of the love triangle. He's got some ideas. But as of tomorrow, it'll be Brad and Hilary and you. Keep your focus."

• • •

Later that afternoon, over drinks at Mirage's Baccarat Bar, Harley and Scott—in a conference call with Amanda Kelly Malouf—amend the contract. Just before Amanda Kelly Malouf hangs up, she advises, "Hold on."

"She said *hold on*. What did she mean, *hold on?*" Scott asks Harley Davidson.

"You need to understand what's happening," Harley answers, "because you're on a ride."

Ride? Where? How? The speed and mutability of the world have Scott more than a bit off balance.

"Look—" Harley begins. "Listen—" He says maybe it's his Scientology talking, but he believes every person has a moment in which opportunity becomes visibly manifest and if that moment's acknowledged—recognized—it can become a lifelong friend. "Why we're here," Harley explains, "why we walked into this bar and sat down and are having this drink, is that today you and Opportunity went toe-to-toe, stared into each other's faces."

On the ride back to his apartment, Scott decides that he'd better at least try to explain some of the strange weather in his life to Tory. He doesn't know what he'll say; he doesn't even know what he'd tell himself, but he commits to an attempt—however stumbling.

But Tory's not home. He's left a note: he's not sure when or if he'll be home. He and some other *Art Dudes* are tagging a building wall in

North Vegas where developer-landlords are forcing Latino families out. *We want to make a statement.* And maybe it will take all night; maybe they'll all get busted, end up in jail; maybe he'll sign the wall, making a big "T" with his cane; maybe he'll sleep over at this other Art Dude's place; *he's got a nice sister and she's into me.*

Scott paces their four rooms, each one of which, even when he's in it, seems empty. Finally, he pours some wine, plunks himself down at the kitchen table, takes out his pocket sketchpad and tries to compose things to say to Tory to explain the sudden shifts and fissures in his life. What he writes down uses a lot of water and wind words like *flow* and *current* and *direction*. He works for an hour, refilling his glass twice, but when he reads what he's written, it all seems like nonsense.

His and Tory's times at home don't coincide for a week. They leave what someone else might judge to be stupid and obligatory notes for one another—references to the *needs of friends* and *not owning my own time.*

Scott finds himself tracking Tory, deluding himself into thinking that because he studies the way his new portraits change from day to day—tiny shifts in the direction of the light source, small mutations of color—he's onto Tory's feelings and thoughts and moods. On one occasion the oil from the day's work is so fresh, the taste of its application so immediate in the room, that Scott swears Tory must have heard his key in the lock and slipped away through the half-opened window, dropping a single story into the shrubs below. But how would a person using canes even begin to do that?

The three *leads* in the film—its working title now changed from *A Taste of Neon* to *A Girl Named Megan*—hang out on the set and become friends. After only a week Scott is calling the other two *Hil* and *Brad*, touching them, joking with them as though they'd all gone to high school together. They call him *F. Scott* because he's *a serious artist who likes to drink.* On a Thursday night, at the end of a day they began shooting at 5:00 a.m., the three decide to go out to the Red Rock Resort, where they sit in the Tides Oyster Bar, do oyster shooters, and agree that each one will tell the others a never-before-revealed personal secret.

Brad Pitt's secret involves a single homosexual experience—freshman year in college. "What I didn't know," he says, "was that a lot of money was riding on whether, if I got drunk enough, I would let this other guy *do* me. This one particular 38DD redhead was being used as bait, and I began to get what was going on." Hilary asks if he was ashamed, and when Brad thinks about it he says, "There's got to be a better word than *ashamed*."

Hilary's secret is that it's possible—*possible*, she stresses—that she killed someone. It happened when she was twenty-six and had driven all night from Santa Fe to L.A. to get back for the start of a film. So she was winding along this mountain road—just a little moonlight—when suddenly, there's this big *thud*. "Like really big," she says. She was tired—in fact she says it makes her tired just to remember it—but she recalls, vaguely, a shape. She didn't think it was a deer; maybe it was a coyote. But it may have been a human shape. "The point is I just kept driving on. I didn't stop; I didn't turn around." She says that when she got to L.A. early the next morning she saw there was a slight crease in the left fender. "I think it's very possible that it was someone camping or hiking or even bicycling," she says.

The other two try to reassure her.

Scott's secret is about betrayal. In his Michigan high school, he'd shared Best Visual Artist status with another student, Kendall Lee. They were both runaway prodigies. One day their art teacher, a man named Christensen, gave Scott a flyer announcing a new full-ride art scholarship to the University of Michigan and asked that he share the information with Kendall. But the temptation to do art for four years—everything paid—had been too much. Scott had copied down the information, then burned the announcement. "Ultimately, I got into U-Michigan...but as the award alternate. Kendall Lee got into Pratt—but he had to take out a lot of loans."

"So our new buddy's a Judas," Brad Pitt says to Hilary.

"Right—and you! You're the name that dares not be spoken!" Hilary laughs.

"So? You're a murderer."

And all three laugh.

Driving home after they've parted, Scott finds it curious that all their secrets were negative. Nobody said: *My secret is that I want to start a foundation for orphaned Sudanese kids.* Or: *My secret is that I want to give up film and devote the rest of my life to Habitat for Humanity.*

Yet again, Tory isn't in their apartment. This time his note says: *Staying over at Ricardo's place on Knotty Pines.* And there's a phone number.

Scott pours himself a drink and again threads a figure eight in and around Tory's portraits, trying to find secrets in what he's done to each of the images in progress. Something about Tory's work seems to be getting darker, Scott thinks. Angrier. The way he's using his palette knife, the streaks of black in the red he's using, the broad strokes of silver—it all seems much more cynical. Is Tory angry? At him? If so, why? Are the deaths of his parents finally catching up with him?

Harley Davidson tells Scott almost daily how his star is rising, what a natural he is, how already there are inquiries (Amanda Kelly Malouf's called him and told him) being made as to when he'll be available for another picture, projects being lined up. When Scott is staggered by the size of his first check, Harley tells him he knows a good financial advisor. "You also need to sit down with Amanda," he says. "I don't mean tomorrow—actually, she's busy tomorrow—I just mean one of these days."

The on-and-off-the-set dynamic with Brad and Hilary takes on a volatility. During the fourth week of shooting, one day Brad suddenly wheels on Scott and calls him a *dickhead*! then slams the heels of his hands hard against Scott's chest. "So you should *like* that," Scott shoots back. The next night, when Scott gives Hilary a ride back to her suite after their shoot, she suddenly cups the back of his head with one hand, pulls him in, and kisses him hard. "I'm sorry. I shouldn't have done that," she says and bolts from the car and into the lobby of her building.

On one of the rare evenings when he and Tory find themselves together, Scott asks his young friend: "If I found a studio/loft for you—I don't mean anything big or fancy—would you like that? I've-been thinking—you know, it might be good, a place of your own."

"Who'd pay?" Tory asks.

"Well, this is going to maybe sound crazy, but I've been doing a movie—I got asked to do a movie—with Brad Pitt and Hilary Swank, and so I'm, you know, making a lot. And I could swing it for you."

"You've been making a movie?"

"Yeah. Bizarre. Weird. The whole thing's weird; it doesn't make sense, but—"

"You mean as in *acting*?"

"Yeah. I suppose. That's what they've been calling it, anyway." Scott laughs.

Tory thinks.

"So—?"

"Well—"

"I mean, it's a thing I could do."

"Sure. Fine. I wouldn't turn it down," Tory says.

So Scott gets Tory a loft on Colorado Avenue, and Tory moves out. "Hey, I'm going to miss you," Scott says.

"Well, you know where I live," Tory says.

• • •

Three days before the end of the shoot, Hilary pulls Scott aside and tells him that she's thinking of forming her own production company. "I'm buying properties," she says. "I own the rights to three Paul Auster and three Don DeLillo novels."

"Good for you," Scott says.

"Right, good for me. But the point is: what about you?"

"I'm sorry."

"What about you?"

"What *about* me?"

"Would you be interested?"

"In—?"

At that point, Leonard calls them back for their next-to-final scene.

Under his breath—as the two are standing in place between takes—Brad tells Scott: "Be careful. Don't get in over your head."

Scott and Tory meet for dim sum at Changs on the first after-wrap Sunday, when— just as he starts sucking a chicken foot, Scott's cell phone vibrates. The caller is Harley Davidson, who's just hung up from a call from Amanda Kelly Malouf. "I have her permission to do this," he says and then asks how soon Scott can be packed for three months of out-of-town work—can he be ready by 10 the next morning? Because just on the basis of a rough cut of *A Girl Named Megan* and Harley's enthusiasm, Amanda has gotten Scott thirteen episodes of *Boston Legal*. His bit is that as a new member of the firm, he'll become a kind of son figure to Denny Crane, played by William Shatner. The pay's great—thirty thou an episode. David Kelley, *Boston Legal*'s writer, loved what he saw. Harley's found Scott an apartment in Watertown—very near the Charles. He's leased a car for him. "Listen, why don't I come by and pick you up around 9," Harley says. "We can sign the contracts; Amanda's faxing them. I'll drive you to McCarran. Do you have something in your mouth?"

When Scott hangs up and tries to explain the whole thing to Tory, Tory just spoons more chili paste into his soy sauce and plucks another shu mai with his chopsticks. When he reaches across the table for it, he bumps one of his walker canes, which clatters with a vaguely hollow rattle to the hardwood floor. "Sorry," he says.

• • •

Scott likes Boston. William Shatner's surprisingly low-key. Each day on the set, he tells Scott Captain Kirk anecdotes, which Scott then emails to Tory, who's a rabid Trekkie. All the insider Captain Kirk mythology seems to move Scott and Tory back into a comfortable relationship. On the *Boston Legal* set, Scott and James Spader get into a practical joke competition involving water balloons, tubs of Reddi-Wip, condoms, and small animals from the Brookline Animal Shelter.

Scott flies Tory out to Boston three times. William Shatner joins them for dinner at Anthony's Pier Four and wanders around the Fogg Museum's glass flower collection with them. "There are glass flowers in many of the distant galaxies," he jokes. Tory gives William Shatner a small oil portrait he's done of him and for him. Shatner's face looks like a moon hovering over an ice field.

A Girl Named Megan is released and reviewers praise it, using the words *quirky* and *off-center*. Scott gets referred to as *a compelling newcomer*, and when Oscar-list time comes, he's there with actors like Toby Keith and Ralph Fiennes with a Best Supporting nomination. The *Boston Legal* crew throws him a surprise party, and he's embarrassed. When the chant goes up—*Speech! Speech!*—what he wants to say is: *This is crazy. I just fell into this. I'm a painter and a teacher.* Instead he says, "What a ride this life is!" which makes people laugh and applaud.

Somehow the Oscar nomination seems to wrench the new comfort in Tory and Scott's relationship back into the self-conscious and the oversensitive. Sometimes Tory doesn't answer Scott's emails. Then he writes abruptly that the new physical therapist he's been seeing has *possibly permanently fucked up* his back. When Scott calls to pursue the news, Tory's obviously turned off his cell phone.

One night after their shoot, Scott shares a bottle of iced Tanqueray Ten with James Spader and rambles on about what he calls *all the riptides in my life*. James Spader talks about how making *The Secretary* screwed up his sex life for at least four years.

As the end of Scott's thirteen episodes approaches, Harley Davidson flies into town and they both sit down with David Kelley and some network suits to renegotiate a contract for the season to follow. "I've got Amanda's permission," Harley says.

"Shouldn't I at least talk to her on the phone one of these days?" Scott asks. "Introduce myself."

"Plenty of time. Hey! You have to feel good about yourself," Harley Davidson says.

"Because it's a law?" Scott replies.

He starts to obsess. He feels he has to do something to turn his relationship with Tory back into what it once was, take it back to where it began. What's the feeling he's after? What's the situation he wants again? Yet another time: he makes lists. He writes phrases down. The phrase *a profound saturation of affection* gets rewritten and rewritten and underlined.

Hilary Swank flies him out to Los Angeles to talk about his committing to the lead in her film adaptation of Paul Auster's *Timbuktu*. "It's about a homeless poet and his dog," she explains.

"So do you want me for the poet or the dog?" Scott asks.

Scott reads and rereads the Auster book. He likes it. He and Hilary discuss the project—how it might best be transferred to film. Do new characters need to be created? Should they get Paul Auster to do his own screenplay? Hilary Swank offers Scott her bed and passion for three consecutive nights, after which she tells him that the energy between the two of them has *too much of a vortex*; it's not good for the project; they need to just be friends. Scott thanks her for believing that he'd make a good homeless poet and flies home.

Though the path is rocky, he makes all the arrangements for Tory to attend the Academy Award celebration—first-class air ticket, tux, room at the Beverly Wilshire, breakfast with a half dozen former *Star Trek* actors. He hires an Alexander Technique healer who everyone-he-talks-to says is inspired.

Four days before the ceremony, Scott flies to L.A. Harley Davidson has obligated him to a series of pre-award events and mixers. "It just makes sense," Harley says, and even though the precise *sense* it makes evades Scott's own fragile clarity, he goes along. Of the four days and seventeen events, he remembers only one moment. It's at the house of someone from William Morris—someone with a name that could be either Irish or Jewish. And he's outside by the pool. At the bar. A woman in her early thirties with red hair who Scott's seen in at least seven movies saunters up to him. She's a famous actress and she slides her enormous tortoise-shell dark glasses down her nose until they rest on the tip, then smiles. "Someone said you painted," she says, then adds, "I paint."

Scott can't discover an answer; he just nods.

"This is a business that'll kill you if you just act," she says. Then she suggests that maybe they can paint together. She says she's doing an endangered animal series and she'd love to have him see it—give her feedback. "This is the best number to reach me at," she says and hands him a napkin with the number written on it. Scott folds the napkin, puts it in his pocket, and signals for the bartender's attention. "Another Tanqueray Ten on ice," he says.

Tory's supposed to arrive at LAX midafternoon on Academy Awards day. Scott's arranged for a driver to meet him at the foot of the baggage claim escalator. He's given Tory the driver's cell number, fearful that his own phone may be tied up. At 4:30 there's a text message from the driver bearing the words *held up* and *tarmac*. By the time Scott connects with the driver, the driver's had three more calls from Tory, which he says were "pretty confused." As far as he can determine, Tory's Delta flight hasn't left the runway in Las Vegas. Scott tries Tory's cell phone himself, but an electronic voice tells him that the person he's trying to reach is out of the area. Scott says, "Fuck!" to the electronic voice, tries five minutes later, and gets the same routine. It's after 5:30 now, and the ceremony starts at 7:00.

Tory's dropped off the radar, and for a while it seems that the driver Scott hired has also drifted away from the radar screen. But he finally calls and says, "It's all pretty much confused, but as far as I can determine, the plane has taken off from McCarran. Should I wait? Should I bring him to the awards ceremonies even if he's not in his tuxedo?"

"Jesus Christ—of course!"

It's 6:22. Scott's head feels like a submerged stump he once saw in the Big Wood River—slippery and bloated, with a brain tangle of black roots. *Fucking Delta Airlines! He should have flown Tory Southwest!* They probably unloaded all the baggage to get the baggage of somebody who never boarded the plane.

And now Harley Davidson pulls the cinnamon-red Ferrari convertible he's rented for them up to the carpet. They get out and a valet whisks the car away. As they walk the red path, Scott tries to focus on the carpet threads. Between the ages of nineteen and twenty-one he worked in a carpet outlet store, and the names of different styles of weaves comes into his head: *Frieze, Saxony, Tapestry*. The hum of voices and traffic is vaguely tidal around him: it washes in; it washes out.

When he gets to his seat, he starts having animal memories: the circus, the zoo. The theater's interior seems overlit. Harley Davidson is all energy and nervous anecdotes about stars. Scott hears an oboe. Then a cello. And now trumpets run scales. Drummers test their brushes. The orchestra warms up.

Scott tries to clear his mind, arrange it like place settings at a table. But he can't. And then the evening's begun—Tory's empty seat beside him like the mouth of a cave. There are awards and speeches, awards and speeches. Famous musical stars—backed up by the swollen orchestra—sing songs that have been nominated. Scott checks and rechecks his watch, his cell phone. It's 8:10.

Then suddenly Jeff Foxworthy, the ceremonies emcee, walks somberly to the microphone. At first, islands of the audience laugh—at the pallor of his skin, the hang of his jaw, the float of his eyes. They presume it's a bit. Who wouldn't?

But it isn't. Can the attending multitude offer up, please, a moment of silence. He feels it's important not to disregard what's happened, and the Academy's president, Frank Pierson, agrees with him. There was an attempted skyjacking, he announces. Two terrorists took over a Delta flight from Las Vegas with the intention of crash-flying it into *the very theater we are sitting in right now.* A passenger on the flight—a young man with a pair of canes—rushed the two men. And the plane crashed in the desert, somewhere northwest of Barstow. *Could we all take a private moment, please—each of us in his or her own way?*

The inside of Scott's head ignites in a wind-and-fire storm. There's a screaming sound like seals being slaughtered en masse on an island that he saw once in a documentary. He feels the caving in of his heart and understands he wants to cry but can't: all his body fluids feel like they've become grit and dust. And then, of course, the minute is over, and the awards are on to the next category.

And then the next, his—Best Supporting Actor—which he wins. He can't rise; he seems to be sinking through his seat, but Harley Davidson grabs him above and below his elbow and hauls him up. People all around him stand and applaud. He's out in the aisle. There's a push at his back and he's staggering forward. Where is he? He needs to reach in his pocket for something—what is it? Burnt umber? He climbs the stairs, caroms off at least two people, stands in front of the microphone. The hall quiets.

"I want to thank—" he begins. Then every word he'd rehearsed leaves him. "Sometimes the people we love burst into flames," he says. "And sometimes the people in flames are ourselves."

He makes his way to his seat. The awards go on. They end. Scott rises, pushes Harley Davidson aside, weaves up the aisle. Hands extend to him in congratulations. He takes none of them.

On the street outside there are tourists, well-wishers. He staggers through them. When he gets to where the night is quieter, he hails a cab.

"Where to?" the cabbie asks.

"Las Vegas," Scott says.

Four hours later he is in his Rainbow apartment where he rummages through unfinished canvasses, all of which are too small. Still, he sets the largest on an easel and gessoes it all over, painting all night until he has a searing portrait—blacks and oranges, reds and greens—of a man in flames, after which he drives to the Orleans, where he tries to imagine the last six years of his life haven't occurred—they were just an errant brain wave.

• • •

Man walks into a bar, sits, orders Tanqueray Ten on ice, drinks it. On the bar a midget plays a miniature piano. And there's an old sea-pitted and corked glass bottle with a genie in it. The genie is laughing.

"So—tell me," the bartender asks: "Why the tuxedo?"

The man shakes his head. Finally, he's crying. "It's because I neglected to change," he says.

Escape Artist

They say it can't be done, but in the end nothing contains us. If we ready our minds and are willing; if we set our hearts, we can escape anything, break out and leave the room empty.

Which is not to claim, mind you, that escape is easy. Rather that if escape is a *need*—beyond any of the collaterals of not-escaping—then first, it can be imagined, then done. *Need* is critical harrowing ache and hunger and want. Talk points any of us in a direction: yes; but it won't release; it won't get you, get me, out.

My parents tell stories: *told*; they've escaped now. The first is: me as an infant, weeks old, unnaturally lashed in the swaddlings of my crib. "You should have smothered!" they said. But *no.* Instead I was *out*, *free*, on my back, mouth closing like a fish, all the feathery bunting ribboned and shredded. "You were so tiny—fingers without nails; still—!" They were amazed. Glad, of course, but dazzled. And I've been getting out ever since.

• • •

I have a friend, a woman whose heart is black at times; others, volcanic red. Cut open, she would bleed all the fiery blood of escape. But, compelled as she always is by the open wound, she will not let herself, finally, be cut open, and it is only at night—letting herself out through house windows, through words and dreams—that she finds freedom and escapes.

And though her husband has no idea, he *senses*, and in his sensing *fears*—all that is her being, her impulse—and so makes more and more stringent rules, conditions, takes greater and more elaborate precautions. She will have *Out*, if this world is kind; but he will have her *In*. And he will win. Because—although clearly not brighter, scarcely matching her in ferocity or heart—he is more diligent, more unbending. He is a container—so contained within that he feels bound to contain others. He uses impatience, guilt, sadness and, above all, injured calls-to-duty. Who could deny him his containment? It is so simple, so pure, so righteously self-effacing. But a True Escape Artist—and I wish this for my friend; I do—will out. Will—one day, finally—be in the unshackled air, loosed. It is a matter of spirit in the end. It is a matter of heart.

• • •

When I was two, a nurse locked me in a closet under a pile of coats. I got out. When I was six, three bullies tethered me with clothesline, filled my mouth with detergent. I escaped, spat the detergent into the sunlight; it turned green in the bright air, hardened into a nugget of turquoise. At two, at six, I had no words, no plan, only knew my need: lift, rise, break out, court the insane in the world—if that's what it took. Some days I would put my shirt on backwards, ask my brother to button it—*all the way! all the way! every button!* And I would be out in seconds—shirt on right, rebuttoned to the neck. "How did you do that?" my brother would ask.

Would I have told him if I'd known? Spoken? Voiced the secret? I suspect not, but who can say?

I would be bad—spill milk, utter vulgarities—so that my father would *march me to my room*. Always, before he got back to the dinner table, I'd be there, seated. "How did you do that?" he'd ask. He was the Escape Artist's audience. I'd smile, spill my milk again. This time, after marching me, he would lock the door. But *again* I'd be at the table. He tried spanking me, strapping me, but the—I believe the word is *alacrity—alacrity* with which I would consistently outdistance him to the dinner table only increased.

For months I could see him brooding, deliberating. When I'd spill milk, say a bad word, my mother would fix him with her eyes, draw breath, press her hand flat against her chest, beseech: "Please,

Fred; don't; please, he's just young." She was trying to remedy the problem. I felt sorry—sad that my mother bore pain for me, enough to speak so bravely past the tremor in her hands. I felt ashamed and stopped. My father watched me. Anticipated. My mother watched my father. Do you know that every kind of food, when chewed, makes a different sound?

But then my need to escape, try/test/extend escaping, overcame my shame, and I began again. Because any gift or punishment untested is a gift or punishment unknown. And this time, when my father seized me, intent to march me, and my mother entreated, "Fred, please," I knew he'd confided a plan of extreme measures—and that he was invoking it.

"Lie down," he said when we were in my bedroom. He pointed to my bed.

I lay down.

He left the room, returned with sheets, which he used to tie me, looping both around the bed frame, double-knotting them. "Can you breathe?" he asked.

I nodded.

"Are you sure?"

I nodded.

He stood, studied me, looked sad, like a person who can no longer abide himself. "I didn't want to do this," he said. "I told your mother it made me feel like a monster and was a last measure. But the measure came. Please: don't make me do it again." And, with that, he left—to find me, when he got there, back at the dining-room table, holding a scoop of mashed potatoes in the air with my fork.

I held it there—between my plate and mouth. I saw my father see me. I saw him stop on the rug. I saw him look at my mother, saw my mother study him. I put my mashed potatoes into my mouth, chewed them, swallowed them. And then I saw my father sit down, pick up his fork, take some mashed potatoes on it, finish his dinner.

• • •

I never spilled milk again or said what I shouldn't. I mean, *at home.* There was no longer a need. I knew. My parents knew. I was an

Escape Artist. The point wasn't to be trouble. Why would a person make that choice? *Trouble* was never my point. Whyever *trouble*? It's just: there was a whole neighborhood waiting: a school, a county, a *world*. I long, now, to speak backwards, across time, and advise my father, bedsheets fisted in his hand, *Daddy, don't. Truly: don't. Truths loom larger than any of us, Daddy—even when we are parents—and there is nothing, at those times, that we can do—however awful or extreme—other than join the audience.* I could not be kept in. And it was important that they know, that they have a sense of what would be my life and would always happen. I could not be kept in.

• • •

I collected hemp and clothesline. Sisal. Towing cable. Tire chain. Certain pawnshops carried handcuffs, and I would bind myself so tightly that I bled, but—can I tell a secret?—blood is only lubrication. If you want someone to get away—make them bleed!

I would wander landfills, find discarded clothes dryers, refrigerators. "Chain the door," I would command my friend Nat Breed. "Chain and padlock it!" At first, of course, it frightened him, so he wouldn't. I had to warm him up with ropes and chains, with a restraint I'd found in a dumpster outside a hospital for old people. "How do you do that?" he'd ask. And then: "So fast?"

"Tighter!" I'd say. "C'mon: tighter!" And Nat would tighten the restraint. Then he'd handcuff me. Then wrap tire chains around my legs. But just as he was finishing the tire chains—around and around—my hands would be there, *with* his: "Let me help you with these," I'd say.

Nat was an ice-skater from a family of ice-skaters. When he was eight, he skated with the Ice Follies, and you would have thought skating with the Ice Follies might have given him a chance. But I'd have dinner at his house, and his parents would correct his words: "Not spaghetti, darling—fettuccini." And after I heard them, I noticed that when he skated his spin was too tight. I saw that what he was doing, really, was screwing *into* himself, when all the time before I'd seen him spinning *out* of himself and had had hope.

So it made me sad—the way it makes me sad that the woman I

know who has the *heart* of an Escape Artist won't escape—sad knowing that Nat would settle always for being an Escape Artist's *assistant*. Still, he helped me get further, quicker—padlocking and chaining me into two refrigerators and a washing machine. One of the refrigerators I had him push over the brow of the hill, down into where the landfill was burning.

"Lou?" he said—standing in the debris at the edge, looking down. "Lou?" And then: "*Lou*?!"

And maybe it was mean—I don't know—but I tapped him on the shoulder from behind—"Looking for someone?" I said. And he screamed and cried, this ice-skater, then started to shake and couldn't stop shaking.

"I'm not doing this anymore!" Nat finally said. And he meant it. He kept his word. Something in him, in the way his family had raised him, stopped him from even being an Escape Artist's assistant.

• • •

Do you know about the *Quem quaeritis*? It's what the angel says to the three Marys when they arrive at the tomb of Christ: *Quem quaeritis*? Whom do you seek? And—I'm not sure which one of the Marys it is—tells the angel: *Jesus*. And the angel tells them, *He's gone; He's not there; He's risen. The stone's been rolled away*. It's true: He's escaped. It's gospel. But it's also this little drama in which, sometimes, there's a scene where Jesus kind of sneaks up behind Mary Magdalene—the way I used to sneak up behind Nat Breed—and they have a conversation in the way that, one day, I have promised myself, I will have a conversation with the woman I know who is contained by things that needn't contain her.

• • •

There are secrets. Tricks. Which I showed Nat. And there was curiosity; the tricks teased him; something in him would catch fire, briefly, with the idea—but then he gave it up. "You did it once!" I'd say; "If you do it once, you can do it again!" But no. Sadly, no. Most people, like Nat, shrink. You demonstrate, draw diagrams, write books—they lean in, then lean out. Or, like my woman-friend, gifted and fully capable, they pat a kitten, go to bed, join a chat room. *If you did it once, you can do it again!*

"No. It was a mistake," Nat would say, seeming angry. Fascinated by escape in *me*—but terrified by its possibility in himself. He wanted no part.

"Nat," I'd say, "there are *secrets.* One isn't simply *born* escaping!"

But he'd turn away, walk to a window, throw a rock at a tree.

There *are* secrets. For centuries secrets have traveled to where any of us stand, stirring the air idly. Swimmers find them sunk in lagoons—more secrets than there could ever be *Keepers of Secrets.* Some of us leave our bodies, descend wells, snake our way out of the mouths of chimneys riding the ghost of discovered secrets. Shark's tooth! Applewood! I mean, what do you think of when you think of *Bethesda, Maryland*? Oh, sure! some say: *Give it up; I can see what you're doing, and it's all arcane*—but when what's most familiar is the dusk, the aquifer, the windsong, how can a person not want his laugh to be the aftermath of a cage? I mean—!

This much I'll say: it's the heart—the heart first. With a proper heart: if you can imagine an unbinding—then you can be unbound. If you have the heart and can imagine—the tricks will work, tricks like blood being lubrication, breath tricks, muscle tricks. Tricks of the eye, tricks of the diaphragm and mouth. All these can be learned and will see you through—if the Spirit of Escape is seated in you; if you desire and can imagine it.

• • •

In high school I escaped from detention and trigonometry. You say: *Lots of people get out of detention and trig in high school.* And that's right; they do. But what I'm talking about is: the school, Patterson High, the teachers: they all thought I was *there.* I got credit for the trig and whatever you get for detention. I passed. One term even with an A.

I got out of a date once—the daughter of some friends of my parents—and she had a great time! I got out of mowing the lawn—my father raised my allowance. You see: they march children to their rooms, but the truth is, parents *want* a world where people get out. It's a relief. It's a consolation.

• • •

I went onstage first at the age of seventeen; it was a Rotary Club talent show. I had the owners of two car dealerships bind me with towing cable and arc-weld me into the trunk of a Pontiac Firebird. The assembled smiled: *The kid will never get out!* But I was standing on the sunroof before the sparks from their welding torches stopped pooling on the linoleum floor. The Rotarians had wanted their own, not some kid-with-a-secret, to succeed. But they applauded anyway. And the more successful dealership owner, a man by the name of Dusty Miller, straightened his hairpiece and offered me a job. "In the best of all possible worlds," he said, "I want Houdini on my side!" I declined.

At Yale I got out of physics and ROTC. I was beyond wormholes and uniforms—pre-med and working on being buried alive. I was an apprentice to invisibility within no time: brother to all Jeremiahs and the Anasazi. Once a week I rode the Amtrak into New York to visit a Chinese apothecary on Pell Street, where I had the tips of my fingers injected with a colloidal dust of herbs, a sheer serum the color of tongues. I would sleep on a small cot in the back room of the apothecary, wake and walk the few blocks to Orchard Street, where I would be given instructions in numerology by a woman who had left everything behind her years before in Rumania. Her neck was like a neck in a Modigliani painting. I asked once: "Might we become lovers?" She said nothing, shut the ancient book, slipped her black wool dress over her head, showed me the crosshatches on her breasts. "These are scars," she said.

I have tried not to abuse that which was given to me—this ability. I got out of the military, but that I neither rehearsed nor sought. And that I eluded the life of a doctor—my father's life—was in no way fugitive. It contained no art, secret, or mystery; it was choice, brute stubbornness, resistance.

I escaped the East Coast, but that was simply American—reflex, not gift: a tic of history. People without the vaguest inkling drift west, desert Bethesda, New Haven. They're everywhere. Countless. Pods and congregations. You will find them in Escalante, Utah, swapping stories at the Burr Trail Café. In Ketchum, Idaho, at the Pioneer—though they dress differently. In the small brothels and casinos and along the Truckee River in Nevada—not exactly, but still in some way *refugees*... from too many expectations.

• • •

By the age of twenty-three—manacled and weighted—I was being dropped from bridges. The Brooklyn. The Sunbelt Sky View in Tampa. The Mackinac. People ask: *Was the water cold?* It makes me grin. It's a question I love. *Was the water cold?* I have no idea because, you see, I don't, as they say, *do* temperature. My belief is: where there are instruments that record or *perform* things like temperature—*fabulous! Let* them; never compete with technology.

By twenty-five, I was being dropped from all the *same* bridges and more—first in trussed alloy coffins, then set in concrete. I'd become a headline. All the wire services sent reporters. They couldn't know that, in the span of merely two years, I'd become ashamed. A famous writer said once: *When in doubt, increase the difficulty.* And that had been my intent, been what, yes, it had looked like—coffins, alloy trussing, concrete. But what you discover is (and it hurts): it's like juggling—you haven't increased the difficulty of *anything*; chainsaws are just *candlepins* with motorized blades. Once you know the essential secret, you can just as well make a sixteen-wheel Peterbilt truck disappear as a silk handkerchief. So you lie stretched out and indifferent in a titanium casket at the bottom of a poured foundation, and you think: *This is wrong! This is idle! This is housekeeping! What I need is accident. What I need is to rip the net from the world—to be caught off guard, swept up in an avalanche or something.* It's that awful moment when any of us realize that why we began something is no longer why we're doing it.

Certainly; true: escape's necessary; I understand that; escape's thrilling. But you can't be heedless—not with a gift—it's wrong. A gift should never become habit or reflex. I got out of a marriage when, possibly, it was the avalanche I needed. One of the last times I was dropped—inside thirty thousand pounds from the Golden Gate—I escaped quickly, emerged unseen, and made my way—dressed, dry, mindless, nearly—to the deck of a tourist ferry filled with watchers intent on the bay where I'd been dropped: waiting, curious, eager, expectant. And I watched them watching for me, for whatever evidence would float up. For my escape. And a feeling I'd never felt—fluid, hot, unstable—rose inside: a sad feeling, sick, a nausea, a vertigo. And it was all about why the people were there and what they were watching for, wishing for, hoping for. And I thought: *I don't want to be who I am.* And then *that* seemed wrong, self-abasing, shameful. So then I thought: *I don't want to be who these people are gathered for—* because I thought I saw my old onetime ice-skater and high school friend Nat milling in the crowd.

Believe: it wasn't easy. I'd defined my life. I was an Escape Artist. I'd spilled milk, spoken heretically, transgressed, unbound myself from the whole world of promises and expectations. Still, I felt, for the first time, misdirected and unsure.

And so, in a blink and spark light, I escaped the deck of that ferry and found myself on a hill in Sausalito, rehearsing the name of the place: *Sausalito... Sausalito... Sausalito.* And from that hill, that place, that *Sausalito,* I looked out. And could see the deck of the ferry I'd just stood on—same curious crowd pressing its rails, looking, expecting me.

And the ferry seemed... *what?* It seemed a craft both so overloaded and so without destination that my breath fled. It was a vessel, true, filled and laden—but it disheartened me. So I turned and moved away. Went. Didn't stop. Didn't look back. Instead: became invisible. Became a ghost anchored only by an abiding faith, finally, in the power of absence.

There are rumors, of course. They come. The twilight bears them; I hear. I catch them dripping from the beak of osprey; they ride on the backs of mink and martin. Gossip of the dredged bay and empty casket. Voices saying that I was never there in the first place. That it was all ruse and sham. Others say that I am now Father of the tide, Brother of the char and salmon.

Let the scandal be, then. I'm away—that's enough. To where the escape plan is different. Simpler. More extreme.

So—if you are—don't look anymore. If you're marking time—don't wait. Don't rely. Don't anticipate. I've left behind iceboxes and spin dryers, chains and restraints, coffins and concrete. I've obliged myself: *Never reappear.* Reappearance only creates Faith. And Faith is what's heartbreaking. Faith is what takes our will away and what makes us cry: Faith that this will go on—love, luck, pleasure, or success. Faith that we can name something *the Future* and, in naming, have it rise up—out of some dark and murky bay water— like a lover gone suddenly silent, and say: *It's fine! Here I am! A child finally of Light and Dark! Both now! Here I am! Let's begin!*

Don't wait. Please! Don't look. How about this! Make *yourself* escape! Make *yourself* reappear! Tap *yourself* on the shoulder—say, *Here I am!*

When the Magician Calls

Everything is appropriable; no one owns anything; there's no such thing as *property*. It's like *history* or fresh produce: we pretend because it's a way of being in public, but at 2 in the morning it's unenforceable. Open the yellow pages. *Title Companies* is the longest section after *Private Escorts* and *Physicians*. *Copyright Law* is a contradiction in terms. A person says, *my home*, but what they mean is the leftover pizza. Another person says, *We have out-of-town guests*; truth is: they're talking about themselves. Anything a person might own trembles under a patina of theft. Every day we divert ourselves with the lives of other people, write them letters, emails, Instagrams, ask: *What is your middle name? Are you ever lonely?* It's all, finally, time-share and real estate. There's never a month when we're not sixty days overdue.

Still—it's hard not to imagine. Or dream. Like *history*—there's desire. I want; I long; I imagine. Like any slap-footed clown, I fall down; I say *mine*.

• • •

A year and a half later, I call Sheila at her home. "Me again," I say.

"I'm sorry: who is this?" Sheila says.

"You don't remember?" I say. And of course she doesn't, won't.

"My breather?" Sheila asks.

"A man said he saw half of you here in Idaho," I say.

"Which half?" Sheila says.

"The beautiful half is what the man said."

"Yes. It would have to be," Sheila says.

"The half that loves stones and shells. Singing."

"Well—certainly that's the half I've not had."

"So it was you?"

"Bet on it," Sheila says. "Because, more and more, I'm useless to myself. Here. On this bay. With Alan. Fact is: we've got it almost perfected—both of us—being useless to each other. Wait—! Something's coming back," Sheila says.

"Having to do with wallpaper?"

"Wallpaper—" Sheila says. And then: "Oh! Oh, *wall*paper: *you*. *Yes*."

"You're remembering," I say.

"The man in the Donna Karan!" Sheila says.

"I confess," I say.

"Are you still a dentist?"

"No. No; I built too many bridges," I say. "Gondoliered too many root canals. There's a statute of limitations on nitrous oxide."

"You're in Idaho?"

"Magic," I say.

"Idaho?"

"How I got here. So—you're intact? Full possession? Own your own life? There on the bay? Back? Not just half?"

"It depends," Sheila says.

"On—?"

"The tides."

"Yes, *tides*, of course; I see."

"And *intact*: what you mean by it."

"No lacerations, though? No scars?"

"Before? You didn't notice my scars?"

"I only saw a woman who was beautiful."

"I think it was a trowel," Sheila says. "Then, of course, much earlier, there was the nail."

Telephones destroy lungs. It's a fact. The industrial disease of telemarketers is emphysema. It's all circuitry and relay. The way they lay their cable—how it beds in the igneous earth. "I have a last question," I say. "Which I need to ask before my *first* question."

"Ask."

"Do you get the stones I send? They arrive?"

"Always," Sheila says.

"Hold them to your ears."

"I have. They sing," Sheila says.

"And you hear?"

"I hear everything. My daughter uses them. Did you know I had a daughter?—yes, of course you did. On glass. Uses them. Goblets of glass. With silver wire and amber. Fastens them. She knows your name."

"How so?"

"The envelopes with your stones."

"But—"

"Yes?"

"I never used a return address. Never have. I wouldn't know what address to—"

"When you add the envelopes up, though—"

"Right; I see."

"It's Lawrence. It's Daniel. Your name."

"Which?"

"Both."

I hang up.

• • •

Again, Sheila's right. *Both* is my name. Has been. Since birth. Parents name their children for what they've lost, and my father lost both of his parents. My mother lost her pride and the ignorance of her brothers. Countless days, I have been in two cities at the same time. Two states is nothing. Here I am in Idaho—but nothing's exclusive; so is it Idaho that I'm in? Any of us are the clothes we wear and what lurks in our belly. Any shape hovering over us in the dark has been sent to end our lives and to begin them.

So: time again, I think, to be criminal. Be the transgressive self that I, most authentically, am. I say this aloud; certain people register alarm. My answer: *Take a moment; think.* There are a dozen egrets on a St. Andrews Beach cypress on Jekyll Island. They're all poised. Sentinels. Who wouldn't think to move toward them? Make them rise and batter the air? Whip the sunset to cyclone? Things-as-they-are are intolerable. We live to violate. Lust for a second chance. Those egrets *need* us. And the too-still air! And the smug, molten light!

What we can't name is photography. Who would simply stand, the night coming on, perfect as it certainly is, and freeze ourselves in a postcard? Things-as-they-are are intolerable.

Criminal, long ago, ceased to be a question of *whether* and became *how*. Sheila lives monitored. Is that just? When the world's kind, during her best moments, only half of Sheila travels or is set free. There is this *gel*—and I find it infuriating—placed by Alan *around* Sheila, of surveillance. And accountability. So: never *whether* but *how*. Last time it was wallpaper. This time—who can say?

Sheila suffers from spontaneous asthma. She never had it—then did; her breath, like extra eyeglasses, suddenly lost. I could pose as a neuro-pulmonary specialist. Demand she participate in a seminal test group. Except I'm tired of medicine. All its carbon chains. How do you rip the wings from egrets and let them fly? No; not *whether*—but *how*.

I spring the gate at a North American Van Lines lot and steal a truck. I drive west, then south. For three days, the huge padded and slatted carapace of the empty truck feels like an unbooked, darkened theater. Just a matter of time—then *Death of a Salesman! Our Town! The Sound of Music!* My stage-self hungers for standing-room-only. Mostly, though, I feel like some kind of bulked tortoise, lumbering to the sea. Which I do. Then, arrived, break Sheila's security code for the second time, watch the Tellers' gate slide wide open.

When the magician calls—who answers? Open the yellow pages. We pretend because it's a way of being in public. Every day we divert ourselves with the lives of other people. No one owns anything. Still, it's hard not to dream.

Such a sweetness, I think, in trespass! Such a truth. I idle the Van Lines truck just outside Sheila's front door. Alan is there. I get out, bigger than myself in my blue moving suit. "Furniture ready?" I say.

"Furniture?" Alan Teller says.

"October 2nd. You would be *Mr. Teller*? I'm here for the furniture."

"We're not moving," Alan Teller says.

"That sounds a bit resistant," I say.

"Produce your manifest," he says.

I do. Manifests are easy.

Alan Teller peruses it. "There's a mistake," he says finally.

"Really! Welcome to the world," I say.

Sheila comes out. She's dressed in a sea-green, almost black dress with red roses. She's barefoot.

"Sugar—put your shoes on," Alan says.

"I left all my shoes in Jamaica," Sheila says.

"She likes to argue," Alan Teller says. "And she has this imagination."

"I like to breathe, too," Sheila says. "But what does it get me?"

"Were you *going* somewhere?" Alan asks Sheila. "*Think*ing you might?"

"Baby, I'm already there," Sheila says. "If you could only track."

Then Sheila has me in her sight finder, sees through my blue coveralls, computes what stands under my North American Van Lines cap. She shakes her head, bites her lip to keep from laughing. She reaches into her shoulder bag, removes a small silver-alloy handgun, extends it to Alan.

"You want to shoot this man?" she asks.

"Not especially. Do you?" Alan asks.

"I thought *you* might," Sheila says.

"Why?"

"Because he's come here to take what you own away," Sheila says.

"I could shoot *myself*," I say. "If it would make loading the van easier. Here. Give me the gun."

I can tell Sheila likes this. She lays the small automatic on her open palm and extends it. I heft it momentarily, then take it in my right hand, place the muzzle to my left shoulder, and fire. Blood begins to seep into my blue uniform. "That help?" I say.

"Jesus Christ!" Alan Teller says.

"Between 9 and 10 at night I walk my dog," Sheila says. "Don't show off. Be smart."

I have Sheila now; she's pissed. "Don't show off?" I tease. "Be smart?"

Her black Lab wanders out the front door. "Bite this man, Homer!" Sheila commands the dog. The lab looks at her—then at Alan.

"Do you know you're bleeding?" Alan says.

Sheila crouches and pets her Lab. "Homer? You looking forward to our walk tonight, sweetheart?" she says. "You want to run? Want to run through the wide world?" Then Sheila kisses the muzzle of the dog, and the dog, Homer, looks to be in love. Yet sad. Sheila rises. "If I could have my gun back," she says. "Now that you've demonstrated that you have no concept of firearms."

I hand it to her. We both smile. I can feel my blood—where it's accumulating at my waistband.

• • •

"There's a clinic at Center Street and Twenty-Seventh," Alan Teller says. "We're not going anywhere. We're not moving."

"Yes—now that I talk with you, I can see that," I say.

"Can you get there?" he asks. "Under your own steam?"

"I like the way you express yourself," I tell Alan.

"And *me*?" Sheila asks.

"I think who you *are* is expression," I say.

"He's a rogue," Sheila says to Alan.

"Possibly—but a *bleeding* rogue," Alan says.

"Yes—but that's what rogues *do*," Sheila says. "That's what makes them compelling—their blood."

"Call the clinic," Alan instructs Sheila. "Tell them to expect a man with a shoulder wound driving a North American Van Lines truck."

• • •

My advice is never elect stitches. Given the option, choose cauterization. Like history or fresh produce—always take the fire before the knife. There's a world of difference. Ask Sheila. Sheila recoils at the word *incision*. "It's unpronounceable," she's said.

• • •

That night, between 9 and 10, my shoulder charred and crisp as a beetle, I haul my van onto the shore road where I know Sheila will be walking her dog. I coast; I roll; I barely accelerate. Then, as through sorcery, suddenly there Sheila is, like a dancer, in my headlights. You can hear the tide and all its ruckus of shells and rocks just beyond the low brake of mimosa. And there's music from my cab radio—k. d. lang flouting all the rules, still bringing all those listening to their knees.

Sheila never anticipates, never looks behind. She only moves like a stripper in the road. I think: in a world like this, why would anyone breathe? The heart, imagining, is smoke. And all that a person might own shudders always under that patina of theft. Still, things-as-they-are *are* intolerable. So slowly, carefully, perhaps for the first time, I roll my pirated van near, nearer, to what could change my life.

Target Practice

The man I learn from drives us from carnival to carnival in a Chrysler hearse with a convertible top. In Futura Bold it says, **Theobold's Body Shop**. He is a man in his mid-forties—trousers of expensive cotton, shirts of silk. He has a different pair of soft leather boots for every day of the month. Between the ages of nineteen and twenty-eight, he was a change-of-pace pitcher for the Cleveland Indians, and he still carries a canvas bag fat with baseballs and a collapsible net boxed with the strike zone. We can be driving along—he'll pull over, get out, slide the net from the back, set it up, heft the duffel, pace the distance, shovel earth so that it makes a mount, and pitch for an hour or two. "Watch how I break inside," he'll say. "I'm an original." Then he'll call me over, as though I am his catcher and we need to be clearer about the signals. "How're you doing?" he'll ask. "You holding up?"

When I was two and a half I almost died. I've read the hospital report. It says, *Tipped over in high chair: accident.* When I was three I almost died again. *Tripped over a breakfront leg.* I almost died three times when I was four. *Fell accidentally from a bicycle with training wheels. Didn't see open refrigerator door. Lost balance on stairs.* When I was five I was taken out of my house and given to another family. *Tried to remove hot embers from the fireplace. Got into kitchen drawer and played with knives.*

"Two irreducible fundamentals," the man I learn from will say, "if you're going to pitch: breaking inside and change-of-pace."

• • •

There are some books—some people call them *studies*—and certain words appear again and again. My favorite is the word *target. It is not uncommon for the target to... In 78 percent of the case studies, the target...* At some point, I guess, I stopped being a *child*, a *little girl*, and became a *target*. When I was eleven I was the *target* of a Sunday school teacher, after that the *target* of boys who asked me out, later still the *target* for needles. And I guess I'm a miracle too. "Young lady, it's a miracle you're alive," a counselor said once. So I'd been a *target of* and *a miracle* most of my life—up until I met the man who's now teaching me.

I had learned to embroider somewhere: a foster home. At a certain point later, I was in a detox shelter and took to embroidering targets. As the man teaching me sees it: my fingers *were* targets—targets *making* targets. I stuck them in the stitching; they bled. The way the shelter ran, you could earn points for things you *owned up to* in group, say, or for the number of days you'd been clean, *major* points for cooperating with drug & alcohol by fingering bag men, suppliers. A certain number of points and you could go out for an hour; more points, two; the highest number, you were called a *trustee* and could go anywhere.

I was a *trustee*—a target *and* a trustee. Different times, I would go out, walk the streets. It was a small city, a place where my almost-dying had brought me; it was in Nebraska. Some people say there *aren't* cities in Nebraska, but that's wrong; there are. I had a favorite dim sum Chinese restaurant, Café Hong, and I would go there, sit in a bamboo circle of steam baskets—har gow and sesame balls, sui mai and chicken feet. I'd spear shiny pastries with chopsticks, sit and read the case histories of other people, mostly women—*targets*—who, like me, almost died.

One early afternoon, the man I'm learning from now came in. The restaurant was uncrowded. He sat two tables away, ordered a mixed vegetable lo mein, shrimp with hot pepper sauce, peanuts. After that he either meditated or prayed. Then he removed a knife from a sheath and cleaned his nails, wiping the knife on a paper napkin.

"Careful," I said.

"Always," he said. He inventoried my table. "Chicken feet," he said.

"Chicken feet," I confessed.

"It's because of chickens that I got my arm," he said.

"Chickens?" I said.

"Right: swinging them," he said. "Around and around—in a crazy windup—it would break their necks."

I think I made some kind of a face.

"I grew up here—out here," he said. "The West Branch, a farm. Growing up, my chore, the way I earned my allowance, was swinging chickens. Limbered my rotator—possibly. Anyway, I loved the sound—feathers pinwheeling in the air. Sound and feel. And so I started to pitch."

Probably I looked stupid, stared with stupid eyes. I'd heard his words but...hadn't, and I suppose my face, somehow, showed it. So he pulled a paper napkin from the napkin dispenser on his table, wadded it, stretched, wound up, threw it at me. "Pitch," he said. "I started to pitch."

"Pitch," I said—sounding stupid—and nodded.

Then he squinted. "Hey—your fingers," he said.

"What?"

"Sorry—but I can't help it; it's the curse of an observant person—they're all prickled."

"Oh, I know," I said. "I do embroidery."

"Possibly," he said. "But embroidery doesn't do that. I've done embroidery. What I'm seeing, I think, you did to yourself."

"You've done embroidery?"

"Needle. Needlepoint. Some. Not a lot; a little. Petit point. Enough to know the whole object is design, but without damage. You forget: I've pitched. I know design; I know damage. Sometimes pitching's design; sometimes it's damage. Often it's both. But it's a choice. Always."

He lowered his face to his cup of green tea, inhaled, sipped some, inhaled again, set the tea down, got up, crossed to me, squatted beside my chair, reached, took my hand, touched my fingers with his fingers. "You don't need to do that," he said, looking at the pinpricks, the red stubble. "It's a choice. You're aiming at yourself. Don't."

He had been a pitcher; I've said; and whatever the Cy Young Award is, he'd been nominated—twice!—and he called those nominations *rewards sufficient unto themselves*. His wife had run away with his catcher. He had reassessed his aims and quit: *somewhere near the top*, he said.

I offered him a small pork bao. I held it to his nose, then against his cheek, and it seemed, for a minute, he might cry. Then he closed his eyes. I waited.

"Why does it seem that you're ready to learn?" he asked with his eyes closed.

"Well—" I began.

"Yes."

"Maybe—"

"*Maybe.* Maybe yes?"

"Maybe because I am," I said.

"Well, I can teach you," he said.

"I believe you," I said.

He peeled the white paper from the bao and bit slowly into the soft dumpling. "This is very good," he said. "This is excellent."

"They make them fresh—every day," I said.

"Wonderful... miraculous," he said. "Can we meet tomorrow—just after noon? Here? Can you put aloe on your fingers and be ready to travel?"

"I can," I said. "I can; I'm a trustee."

• • •

And so: we went from carnival to carnival. And it's true. Because the man I learn from—after nearly eight years of change-of-pace—became a knife thrower. Became a midway man. And I, myself, am a midway woman, a half-breed—*midway. Half Indian, half geek,* he jokes and then winks—as if we only have the power to sort out *truth* from *secret,* as if there's something between us that's a privilege. It's a gentle wink; he's a gentle man.

We share green tea and steamed pastries. And I have learned all about the weighting of blades. I have mastered the carved and helical grip. I have studied both velocity and alloy. He calls it *learning the language of the game*—punctuation of point, grammar of gesture, score of error. I am a novice, though, always still learning. *Serve,* I learn; *prepare; become that which I have never been.* He has advised me: *dissect courage*—labeling his advice part of *the catechism of the knife.* He calls us *co-conspirators,* but he's a man of generosity to a fault. Before we met I was *directionless.*

You're right to question: *What am I saying when I say directionless?* It's a borrowed word. It was in a Social Services report: *For all intents and purposes, the client appears*... [fill in the blank]... *directionless*. What I mean is: I had no comprehension of *next*. I had no *next* moments; obviously no *next* month, no *next* week. There was no *next* place. I had no sense of moving either toward or away, no sense of *occupancy*—myself *occupying*. Nothing about me *took up*—space or anything else. Do you know what I'm saying?

The first time I hid until after closing so I could spend all night in a library and read, the lights I turned on triggered an alarm. Ten minutes later, five guns circled me. *What're you doing here?* the police officer holding the middle gun asked. *Reading*, I said. *The library's closed*, he said—his gun conducting the air. *Oh*, I said; *oh. Shit! I'm in a library*, I thought; *these are police. Search her*, another officer said. Two minutes later they had handcuffed me and taken me into one of the library bathrooms. I can't remember which of the officers said afterwards, *You're very lucky. Because we could prosecute you for trespassing in a civic facility.* From then on, whenever I spent the night in a library, I left the switches alone. Instead I read by candlelight, sometimes setting up a dozen candles.

The man I learn from teaches me, now, how to trespass. "Trespass," he urges. And he throws the word at me with a wicked smile—as though it were round and had little stitches on it. "Think velocity," he hisses. "Think occupy."

I liked the art books best. In my library days. The great big ones—Della Robia and Vermeer. In the middle of the night, lit by wax, all the different colors in the art books moved like skin. Especially the colors of a man who painted names like *Storm* and *Harbor*. His name was *Turner*. Leafing through his paintings was like a hot bath or seeing my body on a warm day in a mirror in a small room filled up with gas fumes. Or like being naked and alone near where someone had just swung the censor in a church, and organ notes still hung in the air and drifted. I liked this painter—*Turner*. Very much. I did. He seemed forgiving. It felt good that he knew all the colors of a bruise but knew, too, when the bruise was healing. Even though he called the bruises names of water—still, I knew.

• • •

Some people, now, will think, *Oh, dear!* or even *Stupid little bitch.* And, of course, I've heard that. *Oh, dear; stupid little bitch spends whole nights in libraries—looking at pictures! Can't read.* But that's not true; I can. I've read a lot. I read, for instance, about a woman living in Berlin in 1943 who sang in clubs. Writing about her voice, journalists used words like *Haunting!* and *Pure!* and *Rare!* and *Remarkable!* All her gowns had targets, stitched from sequins, on them. At the center, always, was the Star of David. The woman's name was Leah, and her friends, the book said, thought her crazy to announce, *Here I am!* to her enemies. So they begged her to *stop.* Begged: *Please.* Then, when she didn't, they stayed away. They were afraid her circles-within-sequined-circles might, somehow, radiate out and include *them.*

But then—and here's the mystery, because no one remembers anything said—but after a while of staying away the friends began coming back. They sat, drank, ate, spent evenings together, claimed their closeness, listened. Armed officers appeared, like, I suppose the officers who arrived at my night library, but the story is: something about Leah's voice—and the hush, the attention, the wine being poured, the simple food shared—stayed any attack. *It was not defiance,* declared the book I read again and again by candlelight: *It was not defiance.* I memorized that: *It was not defiance.* That seemed important.

• • •

A*lways calculate your drift,* the man I learn from instructs me. And I try to.

• • •

Okay: here is what any knife thrower does. First the knife thrower dreams knife-thrower dreams. It takes a while: they slip in; they're deceptive. In the beginning knife-thrower dreams are very much like the dreams you've always had: no particular light, no fluted air, no blood. At first all the familiar people are present too—mixed with all the familiar *un*familiar people. But then the tempo changes. And there's a bluer tint. Or—all of a sudden, there's a Ferris wheel and a dwarf. There will be a nude you've never seen—neck or abdomen smeared arrestingly with blood. These are the early days, weeks, months. This is the beginning.

Also: the knife-thrower silk screens. Posters. They will be heavy with blacks and silvers, Chinese reds. Midnight blues. Figures in the posters will appear to be wearing evening clothes and white gloves. There will be runway lights somewhere and, somewhere else, a rose. If not a rose, a gardenia. If not a gardenia, a cigarette. What's overwhelming is the sense of night, though it's not simply night; it's more elaborate.

As well, the knife thrower meditates. For echoing voluble hours. And the knife thrower is a Feldenkrais practitioner. The knife thrower writes villanelles and ballads—I have begun a ballad with the working title "Song of a Trustee." One of its lines is: *I ship my skin to Portugal.* The knife thrower studies counterweight, learns ballet. The knife thrower is a lepidopterist but only when lepidopterology arises. In this, what is true is *pinning.* If pinning's called for, pinning will take place, but pinning always clothes with a precise care and nomenclature, pinning schooled in the art of prism, pinning informed by the brevity of life and accomplished always through refraction.

Then, of course, there's the Assistant. The Assistant stands...well, you've seen; the Assistant stands always inside the body outline, back to board, in any pitch and spangled carnival night. Calliope music plays. Often, quite near, a spider monkey dances, bounds from the hurdy-gurdy at a string's end and extends his cap. Carved, painted horses lope through the air like pistons, up and down, around and around. And all the while the Assistant stands—patiently and politely. The Assistant waits—familiar with the singing air that has not yet really sung...but will. With all that's Accuracy. With all that's Skill. Because the Assistant is the Assistant, after all, and is beholden.

I am *not* the Assistant. I need to repeat that. I am *not* the Assistant; I've learned this. I am *She Who Learns.* I have been taught that: there is the Lancing of the Skin and there is the Surrounding of All Life, and between these stands an enormous difference. What I want is to possess my body—not to be the locus of misdirected points, embroidery or otherwise. Not to be the target of random knuckles. Not to be the Accident chalked out in outline on the rug. What I am involved in, and perhaps here, somehow, I've misled you, is being Practice and not Target. That's the opportunity that the man I learn from has extended to me. He says, "You will hear the word *arrogant*, and you will hear the word *defiant*. Listen to no one; be proud you're both."

He has never missed. Still, he says, "Nothing deceives more than accuracy. Be vigilant." His dreams, he says, record endless disaster, genocide. "I've chosen a path," he said; "I stand; I calculate—load, lift, hurl—error is constantly within reason."

Error is constantly within reason. His words whistle through the air—there for bloodletting, there for theft. I think I will work them into my next villanelle.

And so—if it is a Tuesday and, say, Moline, I am mindful. In the Indiana dark, I prepare. All-night radio stations play Jewel singing Tammy Wynette. Somewhere a meteor shower gets ready for August. A yellow cat, among chrysanthemums, dreams of towhees and finches.

I love riding in our hearse with the top down, sightseeing with my guide. Across all this continent's between-carnival landscapes, we are, at once, a thing-free and a-thing-that-might-easily-kill: motion and lethal instrument. The man I learn from says, "Every journey is a defiant pilgrimage and undertaking." And I have not found, yet, any reason to dispute this. Then he might reach into this cloth sack he carries, scoop raw rice, withdraw his fist, whip it high into a wild corkscrew wind, opening his fingers like a magician's—hundreds of grains sailing into the world like seeds. "Unless we're careful," he says, "this could be the end of Nebraska!" Or the Sonora Desert. Or Mississippi. Or the Everglades.

I know I've said this, but I am not the Assistant. What I am preparing for—because he is, after all, the Knife Thrower, and the Assistant is, after all, the Assistant—is to be the Blade, the Knife. That's my apprenticeship. That's what—chance constant and time kind—I will become: the Knife. Sometimes I place my hands over an open fire to season them. Other times I lower my face. Flinty sparks scatter past my cheekbones. I try, always, to feel the weight of myself, the balance. A hundred times a day, the man I learn from lifts me over his head so that I can feel—not just on my skin but in my blood and bones—the extension, the load, the cock.

Someday, someplace, I will know gifted hands. Moments of weight will give way to better moments of weightlessness, and for the time that's necessary, I will be pure direction. I will be aimed. I will be just like a windy and held note in the fluted air. Someday—Greater Spirit willing—I will be that tempered thing that could slip between your ribs and into your heart, that which could, oh, so readily, kill you—but doesn't.

Because of the care. Because of the practice. Because of the faith.

The Warren Beatty Project

Things had been up and down for Ethan Weise, and it was hard to know: was the West Coast the best place? California certainly wasn't Wisconsin, where Ethan had grown up. And Los Angeles wasn't Detroit; it wasn't even New York, where he'd studied painting and made his first couple stabs at producing passable canvases. And his half house in Venice bore no resemblance to the house he and Suzanne had been caretakers of for two years, after art school, in Santa Fe. Things felt tricky. Felt, in fact, ungrounded.

Even his personal life felt ungrounded. The Suzanne relationship grew more off than on the wall. On the other hand, he'd exhibited paintings in one group and two individual shows. He had a gallery. He'd sold to people with names. Jeffrey Katz. Lannie Lane. He'd been a "visual consultant" on a short feature directed by a student at the American Film Institute. And there'd been the call from Warren Beatty.

Still: Suzanne moved in; Suzanne moved out; Suzanne moved in again; Suzanne moved out. She'd moved out that morning for the third time. Before the call.

"Can you explain this to me, please?" he'd asked. She'd been wrestling her duffel out the door.

"It feels wrong," she'd said.

"I see. What feels wrong?" he'd said.

"The dust," she'd said. Have you seen the dust in the light? When the sun hits it?"

"No. I'm sorry. I *may* have. I *probably* have. Tell me about it."

"It's *orange*."

"Right."

"And the floorboards are terrible!" she'd said.

"Well, then, you're wise to leave," Ethan had said, pissed. "Orange dust, terrible floorboards: I'd get the next plane, definitely, to Terre Haute."

"Don't be sarcastic," Suzanne had said.

"I'm sorry," Ethan had said.

Suzanne *was* from Indiana. Sometimes that seemed the explanation. *This is Suzanne. She's from Indiana.* He'd met her in Santa Fe, though, and she'd seemed so sweet, so innocent. She even seemed to love him...most times. But she made contact with reality in a language Ethan had either forgotten or never learned. "I went up into the mountains and saw a *bird*," she'd say. "There are birds in Los Angeles," he'd say. "Not *birds*," she'd say, "not...*birds*." She wanted them to live in Montrose, Colorado, because she'd driven through once and had thought it beautiful.

So now Suzanne was *out* again. And here *he* was...in the dusty house with the terrible floorboards. She was gone. He'd stopped asking where she might go, just hung in, waiting for her call. "I'm in Preston, Idaho...on a lake." *Okay.* "Are you jealous?" *Should I be?* He'd imagine her at such times and paint her. Most of his work, in fact, during the last four years, was of motion: mobility, people moving. He'd done a whole series of hitchhikers. Another of people in isolated cafés or sitting on oil drums wearing backpacks in far-off gas stations. He loved Edward Hopper. What Ethan wanted in his own work was to bring Hopper and all his people *outside* and into the light...make them sweat, make them *really* placeless, take their motel rooms and train stations away, *evict* them, put them on the road. The series he was into for the March show was one of twenty to thirty aged backpackers living in city parks.

Then the call came from Warren Beatty.

He'd painted until about 10:00, then watched some basketball, then gone to bed, the bed smelling of Suzanne so that Ethan had felt angry at first, and then alone. But he'd fallen asleep. And then, sometime after midnight, the phone had rung. He'd groped for it.

"Yeah?"

"Ethan?"

"Yeah."

"This is Warren Beatty," a voice had said.

"Right," Ethan had said.

"I was just sitting here with Emilio, and we're talking about your work. Emilio bought one of your paintings. The redhead? In the Levi's jacket? In the back of the pickup?"

Ethan slid awake.

"...and we were just agreeing how perfect you'd be to direct this project."

"Which *project*?"

"This project we're *do*ing,"

Who was this? Ethan wondered.

"Can I send the script over?"

"Sure," Ethan said. *Who the fuck was this?!*

"Then, as soon as you get back to us, we can, you know, hopefully, move."

"Right," Ethan said.

"I'll send it right over."

"Right."

"Be well."

He fell back to sleep. It seemed only moments later that his front buzzer woke him. He got out of bed, looked through his bedroom front window. Parked in front of the house was a limousine. *Fuck!* He threw a robe on and went to the door. A man with long sandy hair and a chauffeur's uniform stood holding an envelope. "Ethan Weise?" he said.

"Yeah?"

"Warren Beatty sent this," he said. He held the envelope out; Ethan took it. "The number to get back to is on the script inside," the man said.

"Sure."

"Goodnight."

Ethan closed the door.

Ethan stood in his living room in the dark, his head slowly clearing. He felt the envelope in his hand, opened it, shook the script out. It felt heavy. Ethan could smell his oils, still damp in the adjoining studio room. He could hear the older Chicano couple in the other half of the house fighting again.

You always out!

You always home!

He went and sat on his couch, flipped on a lamp. The script's leatherette cover was shell blue. Its title was *Hands On*, its author someone named Keithly Pratt. On the lower right-hand corner was stamped: PROPERTY OF WARREN BEATTY/POSSIBLE PRODUCTIONS.

So the call had been real. What was going on? Why had he been sent the script? He was a painter, not a film director. His head felt like he was on amphetamines. His phone rang.

"Hello?"

"Ethan, it's Warren. It's Warren again."

"Hi."

"You got the script."

"I did. Yeah."

"Just checking. Call me in the morning, okay?"

"Sure," Ethan said and hung up.

• • •

He stayed up and read. The script was 160 pages and terrible: the pretentious philosophical, psychosexual ramblings of the main character, probably the scriptwriter, a man in his early thirties named Parnell. Parnell visits his dying father. They argue. He sleeps with woman after woman is his hometown and abuses them with self-pitying bullshit. He vaguely plots the murder of his father's GP, who'd possibly prescribed a wrong medication a year and half earlier. He repeatedly walks out of the room on his crying mother. He berates his brother for passivity, sleeps with his brother's wife, of course abusing *her* with self-pitying bullshit.

It was terrible!

It was dreadful!

It was advanced-pretentious!

Ethan's phone rang. It was 3:00 in the morning. Ethan let voicemail pick up. It was Warren Beatty again, wondering whether Ethan might have stayed up to read the script and saying he'd check back later.

What *would* Ethan tell Warren Beatty? Jesus! Did Beatty have any idea how bad the script was? Maybe not—he'd bought it. Was Beatty planning to play the character Parnell? Or was that Emilio? And was Emilio...Emilio Estevez? And so, then, what was *their* relationship? Wasn't Emilio Estevez the son of that *other* actor? Sheen? Martin Sheen? Or was that *Charlie* Sheen? Or was that both of them?

Ethan slept for two hours. He got up, made coffee, drank cup after cup, reread the script, wished that Suzanne were there so that they could talk, so that he might use her as some kind of sounding board. Had Warren Beatty said...had he been interested in Ethan to *direct* the film? A feature film? Well, yeah, okay: he'd advised *visually* on one *student* film, but... Still, Warren Beatty had seemed pretty clear that Ethan was *basically* a painter.

The phone rang again just after 10:30. *Again!* Again, Ethan made no move. Again it was Warren Beatty. Warren Beatty said: "We'd really like to put this together. Call me."

Ethan read the script one more time. It got worse. He called Warren Beatty.

"So are you on board?"

"I have reservations."

"Of course! Of course: that's why I sent it over! Jesus Christ, man!" Warren Beatty suggested that they get together for dinner that night at Mason's on San Vicente Boulevard in Brentwood at 9:00 and *go beyond their differences.*

Ethan said okay.

He dressed three times, each re-dress a different image, each time hating his look more. What would Suzanne think?

When he got in his car, he found some drunk had heaved in it. He washed it out with dishwasher soap and warm water, but it still reeked. He drove the Ventura Freeway with all the windows open and got to Mason's late. Warren Beatty was there. And Emilio Estevez and Rosanna Arquette and a blonde Ethan didn't recognize. Mason's was filled with familiar faces. There were so many faces from movies that they blurred and tilted.

Ethan introduced himself. Everyone introduced themselves. The blonde's name was Headley Brent; she'd just been in a slasher movie that Ethan had never heard of. "I love your work," she said. "Do you do commissions?"

"I have occasionally," Ethan said.

"Could you do me hitchhiking outside Barstow in the nude?" she asked.

Anjelica Huston came over, gave Warren Beatty an open-mouthed kiss: they both laughed. "Me too?" Rosanna Arquette said. "Why not?" Anjelica Huston said and did it. "Gross!" Headley Brent said, and everyone laughed.

"Order the shark!" Warren Beatty told Ethan.

He did. He still had the script in his hand. He set it under his chair. Emilio Estevez poured him some wine. "So are we doing this?" Emilio Estevez asked.

Ethan watched Anjelica Huston leave and Cyndi Lauper arrive. Warren Beatty put a hand on Cyndi Lauper's thigh until she slapped it away: they both laughed. "Will you call me sometime?" Cyndi said to Rosanna Arquette. Rosanna Arquette said she would. "Yeah...you *say* that, but you never do," Cyndi Lauper said. "Hey, I *will*," Rosanna Arquette said. "Okay?" and Cyndi Lauper left. Everybody drank wine and talked about agents. The words *asshole* and *sleazebag* were repeated numerous times. Something was happening under the table between Warren Beatty and Headley Brent. Ethan's shark arrived.

"We've got to be somewhere," Warren Beatty said, rising and grabbing Headley Brent's hand. "So you think it's possible?" he asked Ethan.

"It's pretty overwritten," Ethan said.

"Hey, you think that piece of shit's overwritten *now*, you should've seen it when I first optioned it: *217 pages!* I'll talk to you in the morning." Warren Beatty left.

"He loves your work!" Rosanna Arquette said.

"I'm a painter," Ethan said.

"That's what she means," Emilio Estevez said.

"But he was talking about my *directing*." Ethan retrieved the script from under his chair and waved it.

"You have a brilliant eye," Rosanna Arquette said. "That's what matters."

"Warren went out today to Kondelli's, to your gallery, and bought three paintings," Emilio Estevez said.

"We have to be going," Rosanna Arquette said. She kissed Ethan on the right side of his face. The kiss was wet.

"Right," Ethan said. "Take care."

Emilio Estevez stood up and offered his hand for a high five. "Do this project," he told Ethan. "I'm serious. Do it. It can be fucking great."

"I'm—"

"I know what you're going to say!" Emilio Estevez said.

"What am I going to say?" Ethan said.

"*Say* it."

"I'm thinking…"

"Exactly!"

"I'm thinking about it," Ethan said.

"*Exactly!*" Rosanna Arquette and Emilio Estevez smiled at each other. Ethan watched them go.

A beautiful black-haired woman in a sheer blouse, no bra, came over. She sat down. "What're you eating?" she said.

"Shark," Ethan said.

"Can I have a taste?" she said.

Ethan gave her a taste.

"Are you *some*body?" she asked him.

• • •

Early next morning, Ethan called Suzanne's home in Indiana to check whether her parents had heard anything. Was she there? They hadn't; she wasn't.

Just before noon, Warren Beatty called again. He was in New York. "I've got a suite at the Ritz Carlton," he told Ethan. "I've called Frank Pierson, who did *Presumed Innocent.* Just did *Ain't That America.* It's not out yet, but I want the two of you to do whatever you have to to get this dog in shape. I'm sending the plane tickets by messenger. They'll be right over."

"Thanks for the dinner."

"Is round-trip first class all right?"

"It's—"

"Buddy, please. Come on, I'm in a hurry."

"It's fine."

"So, you on board?"

"I'll…"

"Hey, come on, don't bullshit me. Are you on board or not?"

"I'll do what I can to help." Ethan was feeling loony, not sure precisely where his words came from.

"Great. That's perfect. I'm a happy man. I'll probably see you tomorrow."

"Yeah." Ethan set the phone down, stared off across the small living room. Some frangible object crashed against the common wall and voices rose in Spanish. The noon sun slanted in through the high windows. The dust it highlighted looked orange.

He packed his bags and waited for his plane ticket. While he waited, he wrote a letter in case Suzanne returned while he was away.

Dear Suz:

A curious thing. I guess an opportunity. Warren Beatty asked me to direct a film. To star, I guess, Emilio Estevez. The script's not great. It needs work. Emilio had bought one of my paintings and Warren saw it and bought three of his own. I guess they liked the feel or images or... I don't know, visual sense or something. At any rate, I'll be at the Ritz Carlton, in New York, for an indefinite time, with Frank Pierson, who wrote Presumed Innocent. *He also just did* Ain't That America. *I don't think it's out yet. But we're going to work on the script. So if you find this call me at the Ritz. I always miss you when you leave. I'm always happy when you come back.*

Love, E.

• • •

When Ethan finished the letter, he took it upstairs and set it in the middle of their bed, then stared out his window to where the street came and went, mostly with fringe people. He went downstairs. He paced. He went into his studio and eyeballed the unfinished canvas blocked in; half painted a guy in a down vest, standing under a viaduct in some city. What was this whole thing Ethan had with motion?

Ethan waited all afternoon. No tickets came. He called Warren Beatty's number and got someone who said *Mr. Beatty would return the call as soon as he could.* "Just tell him... I may have been confused as to when to expect the tickets," Ethan said.

Ethan waited another hour. He called out for Chinese. He poured some tequila over ice. No tickets came. No one called all night. No one called the next day. No one called the day after that. No one called all week. He kept calling Warren Beatty's number and leaving messages. The woman who took the calls was always polite and nice.

It was hard to paint. Annette from his gallery called to tell him she'd had a run on his work: when would he have more? "I think it's Warren Beatty," he told her.

"Well, there was somebody in a chauffeur's uniform who bought three," she said. "And then Frank Pierson bought one." Ethan said he'd get work over as soon as he could.

Christine Lahti called. She said Warren was going crazy with some personal things but hadn't forgotten about him or about the tickets. "He says: *Just hang on*," she told him and then asked whether he was hungry. It was 10:00 at night.

"I'm not *un*hungry," Ethan said.

Christine Lahti told him she was starved, that she'd love some calamari pasta, although she really shouldn't because she started shooting in two weeks: would he meet her at Matsuhisa on La Cienega? He said okay. They met. She was casual. He was overdressed. She was wearing dark glasses and a scarf over her head. "It's my disguise," she told him. "It's my peasant look." They had the calamari pasta and a really nice pinot grigio.

Ethan asked Christine Lahti what she knew about the project.

"I know it's on," she told him, "that's all. Your paintings are incredible." He thanked her.

Randy Quaid came over and asked Christine Lahti if she'd seen Paulina Porizkova: "She always gets the fucking restaurants mixed up!" he said. "Drives me fucking crazy!" He shook hands with Ethan. When he left the table, Christine Lahti started crying.

"What?" Ethan said. "What? What is it?"

Christine Lahti said that it was nothing. It was just...a thing. It was an old thing having to do with Randy Quaid: she didn't want to talk about it, and she was sorry.

• • •

The next day Suzanne called and said she was in Moab, Utah. "It's incredible," she said. "It's really beautiful. It's the most beautiful place I've ever been."

Ethan considered telling her about the Warren Beatty project but decided against it. "*Come back*," he said instead.

"Do what?" she said.

"Come back," he said.

"To what?" she said.

"To me," he said.

"I feel *you* left *me*... spiritually," she told him.

He didn't have a real way to argue. *She* asked *him* to come to Moab. He said he couldn't just then. She asked why. He said it was difficult to explain. She said the rock was *orange* there. He told her she'd said the *dust* was orange in their half house: what was this thing she had with *orange*? She told him he didn't use enough of it in his work, and when he did it was wrong. She quoted Rilke to him: *Dance the orange!* What the fuck was that all about?

They hung up. Ethan took his shirt off and lay down on the floor. He fell asleep and dreamed he'd gone to Moab, and the two of them, Suzanne and he, were on big rocks, these huge sandstone rocks, and in this place she called the Devil's Garden. The dream was amazingly sexual. He was crazy in love with Suzanne, just wanted her like a lunatic. And everything was very wet and viscous and, it seemed, drenched in fruit. And lots of sun. When he woke, Ethan saw that he had *burned* his shoulders and face, probably from the carpet.

• • •

Warren Beatty finally called, apologized, said someone close had been picked up two weeks before at Studio City on a sodomy charge and *it had been a mess*: Ethan should be patient. Frank Pierson also had a crisis. Things sometimes took time. Would he come over to Warren's that night? Warren had a surprise for him.

"What time?"

"Any time. Come after 1:00."

"Where do I go? How do I get there?"

"I'll send somebody over."

Just before 2:00, a white limo pulled up. The driver was silver-haired and pockmarked and said he'd had trouble finding Ethan's house: he didn't get many occasions to come to that neighborhood. Ethan had treated himself, shopped. He'd put on soft Levi's, a cashmere shirt, and a light tweed jacket. He didn't smoke, but he bummed a cigarette from the driver and smoked it on the way.

Warren Beatty had obviously raided the Kondelli Gallery. He'd taken all the furniture out of one immense room and was having a *showing* of Ethan's work. Annette Kondelli, looking happier than Ethan had ever seen her, wearing something pieced out of angora and silk, her hair metallic and explosive, rushed up. "Isn't this exciting?" she said. "Isn't this incredible? We've sold everything!"

"Surprise," Warren Beatty said.

"Surprise!" all sorts of people said—Elizabeth McGovern, Kevin Bacon, Meg Ryan, Teri Garr. River Phoenix was there. Julia Roberts seemed pissed off and just sat, staring out of a glass wall toward the lit pool. John Cougar Mellencamp *loved* Ethan's work. Most of the Dead were there. People were pretty stoned. Annette offered him a line. He turned her down. He met people. Two producers named Roth. Ridley Scott, the director, who had bought one of the hitchhiking paintings and loved it. Michael J. Fox, who asked him if he was coming out with anything. Ethan said no. "Well, I love your work anyway," Michael J. Fox said. "Which work?" Ethan asked him.

Ethan circulated. A movie was being screened in Warren Beatty's theater. Christine Lahti pulled him aside. He thanked her for the calamari pasta. She said, "Can we talk?" and led him outside, where she told him about a crisis she was having with James Woods. She cried and railed about Phoebe Cates who, she said, was the person responsible. She began heaving with sobs. "Christine..." Ethan said. "Christine, hey!" Ethan didn't know what to do. He took hold of her gently, but Christine Lahti started biting his shoulder through the light tweed and cashmere. "Take me home?" she said. He had no car, he said, and she just walked off.

He went back inside. Jodie Foster found him. "First: I bought one of your paintings," she said. "I love your work, but that isn't what we need to talk about. What we need to talk about right now is: I hope you didn't believe anything Christine just told you. She lies. It's pathological. She wouldn't know the truth if it went down on her. I'm sure you've read about it." Ethan said he hadn't. Jodie Foster said it was in all the *sheets.* "So you're going to start directing," Jodie Foster went on. Ethan said he guessed so. She asked him what made him think he had any talent. He said, "I'm stumped. You tell me." She walked off.

Tom Hanks and Bill Murray were doing a vaudeville bit in the kitchen; George Segal was playing a banjo. Ethan found Warren Beatty and asked about a ride home. "I'm insulted!" Warren Beatty said; "I set up a surprise party, and what do you do?!" Then he laughed. He said: "Air tickets tomorrow!" but told Ethan he'd switched from the Ritz Carlton to a house in Key West. "Fully staffed," he said. "You'll get much more done." Phoebe Cates was pulling on Warren Beatty's arm: "C'mon, c'mon," she was saying, "you promised!" Before Warren Beatty got pulled away, he told Ethan he'd gotten Monte Merrick instead of Frank Pierson to work with. "Frank's up to his ass," he said. "Monte did *Alive*, and he's been asked, possibly, for a polish on Ollie Stone's *Demolished Man*...which hasn't been produced, but will be absolutely fucking amazing. I thought about Judy Rascoe, who did *Havana*, but she's a woman—right? So..." He threw Ethan some car keys. "It's the dark-blue XL by the tennis courts," he said.

Ethan wandered around until he found the XL. As he was backing out of the driveway, a woman in a black off-the-shoulder dress and too much jewelry ran across the lawn. She was barefoot. "Wait! Wait!" she yelled. "Can you take me home?" She said she was Elena Cantata. "I was introduced in *Spike of Bensonhurst*," she said. Ethan apologized; he wasn't familiar.

"I've seen *you*," Elena Cantata said.

"Where?" Ethan said.

"Inside," she said. She said she lived in Santa Monica, so did he want to go to Opera first? She'd heard it was open all night. Ethan said he was tired and didn't think so; another time maybe. Elena Cantata said that one of the Roths had been trying to get in her pants all night, that Daphne Zuniga, *of all people*, had put a move on her, that she was supposed to have left with Tom Berenger but he was fucking Kim Basinger or maybe it was Julianne Phillips in some coat closet—though maybe, actually, it was Kevin Bacon with Julianne Phillips or Kim

Basinger...maybe Tom Berenger had gone home, maybe it just *seemed* like Tom Berenger and Kim Basinger were fucking in the coat closet.

"Maybe it just *seemed* like a coat closet," Ethan said.

"But...Berenger/Basinger! Can you believe that?"

Elena Cantata lived in a small beach house. "I'm renting," she said. She asked Ethan to walk her to the door; she said she had agoraphobia and freaked out between the circle drive and the front door unless someone was with her. And then she asked him in. He said no, but she said she had claustrophobia, "or *dark*ophobia or *something.* I go crazy until I turn on the lights." Inside she left the lights off and kept saying: "Just a minute...just a minute" and fumbling with her purse. Finally she grabbed Ethan and pulled his head down and kissed him, nearly putting her whole head inside his mouth. He felt her tongue slip something under *his* tongue, felt the thing, *whatever*, dissolve, nearly choked, swallowed. Then *something* happened. His head was so ripe he couldn't tell what it was. It was sex or *like* sex or like a *film* of sex—all full of glide and music and airbrush and dissolve.

When Ethan woke up, he was nude and in a hammock outside on the redwood deck and whatever-her-name-was was inside on the couch. He found his clothes, Warren Beatty's car keys, and drove home.

• • •

Suzanne was there. The sun was just hitting the rooftops: Suzanne asked where he'd been. He asked if she would she let him get some sleep, because she wouldn't believe anything he might say, and he was about to become a zombie. She asked, "Are you seeing someone else?" He said he was seeing *everyone* else...but he would tell her about it later. "Whose car is that?" Suzanne asked.

Ethan said, "Sleep with me. Sleep with me. Stay with me while I sleep. Please."

Ethan slept until 5:00 that afternoon. Suzanne had gone to the Oriental market and made a wonderful brown rice and tofu salad. She brought it to him on a tray in bed.

"Did some tickets arrive?" he asked. "Some airline tickets? To Key West?"

"Nothing arrived," she said. "Just me. I arrived. Did you remember that?"

"I did," Ethan said.

"Oh...except someone came and drove away in that car," she said.

Ethan said it wasn't his car anyway; it was Warren Beatty's.

"What did you do to the dust?" Suzanne asked.

He said, "What do you mean?"

She said, "It's silver."

He told her the whole story about the Warren Beatty project. Suzanne said it was interesting. He told her if Christine Lahti called to just say he'd gone out of town. She asked what was he going to do now that he didn't have any paintings left. He said he would deal with that eventually.

She asked: "What if this is *eventually*?...I think *most* moments are *eventually*. I think our time in the Devil's Garden was *eventually*."

"Excuse me?" Ethan said.

"Ethan?" Suzanne said.

"'Our time in the Devil's Garden'?"

"Yes."

"But that was a *dream*," he said.

"Perhaps. For you," she said. "I think right *now is eventually*. Look out front!" He looked out front and saw a U-Haul. "Everything that I own is in that U-Haul," Suzanne said. "I've been packing while you've been asleep. Now it's your turn...or it isn't," she said. "You decide."

Ethan said he would have to wait at least until he saw how things were going to turn out with Warren Beatty.

"That's fine," Suzanne said. "That's your choice." She spooned another bite of rice and tofu into his mouth, kissed him on both eyes, picked up her purse, and left.

Ethan heard an engine start, jumped up, and looked out to see the U-Haul van heading down the street. He threw the window open. "*Wait*!" he yelled.

• • •

Ethan kept running into people at different places. He ran into Teri Garr at lunch one day at Tuttobene. She was very nice. "You okay?" she asked. He said he was fine. She said, "You look blue." He said, "That happens." She said, "How's your work coming?" He said it was in transition. He told her he'd moved to Topanga Canyon and asked if she ever ran into Warren Beatty, if she ever saw him. "Everybody sees and runs into everybody," Teri Garr said. "That's the business. And when you can't find people to run into and see...you *paint them in*, for godsakes!" She laughed.

He kept calling Warren Beatty and getting the nice woman. Getting several nice women, actually. But Warren Beatty never called back.

The Weight-Loss Performance Artist

Ginger's twenty-seven and has almost perfected invisibility. She weighs 340 pounds, is five feet five, and is in the Crossroads Mall, coming from the food court, when two men, Clay and Waldo, ask to talk. She wonders how they've seen her. Of course, she's spotted *them* with their fancy video equipment more than a hundred feet away.

"Hey!" each says, extending a card. *Clay! Waldo!* And then: "Have you ever been chosen for something really important?"

At first Ginger is hesitant. Because—isn't she, at least, *transparent*? It would seem not, because nearby others have begun to stop and watch. She can feel their eyes; she can feel the presences of them float and mill. And, as well, she can feel an emanation, a force that approaches heat, from the cameras. She doesn't like the moment. She feels herself, in part, a sideshow Fat Lady—a celebrity/freak. She can pick out a kind of insect buzz of low words and laughter. It's the sort of discomfort that had launched her invisibility imaging nearly three years ago.

What's particularly strange is that Waldo and Clay seem genuinely happy to see her. Chances are, it's their equipment, but somehow Ginger begins to feel almost special with them.

The two men introduce their gear—its capability, its sophistication. The words they use make her feel like she's watching *Nova*. *Pixel* is their favorite. One says, then the other repeats: *pixel projection* and *pixel predicta*bility. Their voices shuttle like gamecocks or perhaps two lounge-show comedians. The shorter partner, Waldo, keeps connecting the word *chosen* to her. The taller and more red-faced partner, Clay, keeps promising that "in just a minute we're going to show you some amazing pictures we just took."

The word *pictures* frightens Ginger. Her mind swipes at it like it's a mosquito, but like a mosquito it keeps coming back. She tries ridicule: *pictures*, she thinks. *Of what? Of thin air?!* But with the two men, Waldo and Clay, clattering on, neither her swipes nor her ridicule work.

"And—!" each time Waldo inserts.

"And—! Right! *And*—! We're going to offer you a lot of money."

"A *lot*! Because—!"

What their technology enables, they explain, hooking up the word *image* in three different ways is: *image assessment! image enhancement!* and *image predictability!*—all according to supplemental information fed into the camera.

"For example, *age*," Waldo says.

"Or *height*," Clay almost instantly appends.

"For instance—!"

"*Whoa*! You are going to *love* this!"

"—We can take a twelve—year-old boy—say one with a growth spurt and who's shown basketball talent—and the camera will *tell* us—"

"*Forecast!*"

"—With a 97 percent certainty—"

"—What he'll look like at, for instance—"

"—Pick a number!—let's say twenty-three."

"Make it *younger*."

"*Twenty*."

"So that a basketball coach at, say—"

"Duke."

"—Duke! Perfect! Coach K will know whether the kid is potentially someone to keep an eye on."

Today's pixels are tomorrow's reality, they explain. Then they produce her own pictures.

And Ginger begins to first sweat, then shake.

The first image reminds Ginger why she never looks in a mirror. It's huge, swollen, freakish, humiliating. She feels the encircling crowd the way she sometimes feels heat exhaustion.

"Think of this as *Before*," Clay announces.

"The point is we have to start somewhere," Waldo says.

And though the next image, in its way, is again hard for Ginger to confront, it's better—less misshapen, less obese.

"This is you 20 pounds lighter," Waldo says.

"In each successive shot, Ginger recognizes herself, feels herself becoming more tangible, because each image sheds at least 20 pounds. In the sixth photo image Ginger sees herself at less than 200 pounds, and in the eighth at only 152. At 112 in the tenth image, there's no question: Ginger is both clear and palpable, shaped and beautiful.

Someone in the crowd around her prompts a wave of applause, a cascade of claps that travels from the polite to the appreciative.

"Previews of your life to come," Waldo says.

Clay shifts to shots in 5-pounds-less increments. At 105—dressed in the clothes she's dressed in now, shrunk by the technology, of course—Ginger looks, she thinks, like a movie star. "Oh, my heavens!" she says. And then tries to say the next thing waiting in the heated rush of words inside her but can't.

Clay and Waldo pitch their offer. What they propose is that she become a spokesperson for their new and powerful diet product. They keep coupling the words *you* and *perfect* and keep using her first name.

If she'll agree, they say, to sign all the necessary papers she'll be given $4,000 for every pound she loses using their product. They tell her their company's name is PoundSolve.

"Pounds dissolve!" Waldo helps her.

"Sounds like Pine Sol," Ginger says.

Waldo says, "Cute."

Clay says, "Clever." Then he inserts, "Only a few conditions."

Waldo goes on. "Ginger," he begins. He tells her payment will be withheld until the one-hundred-pound-loss mark.

"That's the *bad* news," Clay smiles.

"Hardly bad news, though, because—"

"—If you do the math—"

Waldo leans in, whispers. "Your fist check's going to be cut for about a half million."

Even invisible, even as a ghost only, Ginger needs a wall, a chair, at least, to lean against. "Can you wait a month or two?"

Ginger notices the crowd, which seems to have gathered, in ways, *because* of her. She's failed; she's no longer invisible; she's been seen! She thinks: *How large their eyes are! How many mouths are open!* There are perhaps seventy onlookers now.

They're sure, Waldo and Clay say, that she can understand why their company's reluctant to pay, say, $80,000 for the loss of a mere twenty pounds. *No*! What their company is after is an agreement highly beneficial to *both* the poster/spokesperson and itself. None of this will interfere, Clay says, with her regular day job—that is, if she has one.

Ginger scrambles. Her mind races. She asks what she hopes isn't a stupid question: "Should I get a lawyer?"

At first Waldo and Clay are silent. Then—

"Hey—a lawyer would be fine," Waldo says, "if you think you need one. Sure. Why not? Go for it!"

"Go for it!" Clay repeats.

And then Waldo offers to get a lawyer *for* her at their company's expense. And though she works as a legal assistant in a large law firm, overwhelmed by a grab bag of embarrassment, elation, and disbelief, she accepts.

"We don't want you to rush into this," Clay confides.

"Listen: I tell you what," Waldo suggests. "Why don't we draw up some paperwork, then you can look at what we've drawn up and decide."

"How's that?" Clay asks. "In fact—! Trying to anticipate things—!"

The two produce a document. It runs to two and a half pages—big print.

"This doesn't look particularly complicated," Ginger says, perusing. "It's pretty much what you said."

"Ginger—hey, it's your call," Waldo says.

Ginger signs, loses twenty-two pounds the first week, feels at least her hair's returned to visibility (possibly her smile too), and gets a nonnegotiable check for $88,000. The sight of the check, the feel of it in her hand, takes her breath away. "Put it in a safe place," Clay advises.

PoundSolve's offices—where Ginger goes to pick up her checks and be photographed—are in a strip mall southwest of the city's downtown. Waldo calls them *suites*—three interconnected and heavily carpeted rooms. "Welcome to *company headquarters*," Clay says the first time Ginger visits. There's not a lot of furniture, but it's nice. And there are pictures of movie stars on the walls—mostly Elizabeth Taylor and Kathy Bates and Oprah Winfrey, together with framed articles about them from tabloids. "It's our People of Fame wall," Waldo remarks. "We just love people who are very visible."

The PoundSolve plan involves the following steps. Mix the morning PoundSolve powder with enough water to give it oatmeal consistency; heat it up; add raisins; eat it with 1 percent milk. Mix the lunchtime PoundSolve powder with enough water so that it can be formed into a large patty; fry the patty with no oil in a nonstick pan; eat it in a half slice of pita bread with chopped onions and mustard. Mix the dinner PoundSolve with only enough unsweetened apple juice to shape it around the synthetic turkey bone; cook the turkey bone in the microwave for three minutes (or until chewy); eat it with the PoundSolve mashed potatoes and gravy mix and one packet of the dried cranberries. In addition drink twelve full eight-ounce glasses of water every day. Four times a day with water, take one package of the PoundSolve supplemental vitamins.

"I was never hungry," Ginger tells the two men at the end of the first week.

"And that's the magic!" Waldo says.

"But how could that be?" Ginger asks. "Eating only—"

"That's the secret," Clay says.

The second week, Ginger loses only seven pounds and feels discouraged. But when she arrives at PoundSolve's corporate headquarters and both Clay and Waldo keep delightedly saying, "*Look at you!*" she feels much better. In the photography stint, they keep repeating *Amazing*! And of course the nonnegotiable check for $28,000 lifts her spirits and makes her feel visible as well.

• • •

At her legal assistant job in the sprawling downtown law firm, Ginger has almost electric surges of new energy. "More work—more work," she keeps pleading and notices various eyebrows rising. When they *give* her the work and she *does* it, they compliment her on its quality and accuracy. "Are you losing weight?" a couple of the junior partners ask. *Good Lord, Good Lord: they noticed.* She feels fabulous!

• • •

In the third week, she loses twelve pounds; in the fourth, fourteen. Now Ginger has four nonnegotiable checks from PoundSolve totaling $220,000—enough to buy a house outright. And even better, she's more than halfway to having the nonnegotiable checks become negotiable. She's lost fifty-five pounds! She buys some cherry-red lingerie at Lane Bryant and fantasizes about making a sex video.

When she picks up her fourth check and poses, Clay and Waldo announce, "Ginger, we're ready!"—by which they mean that in the next week ads will appear nationally carrying her first four weeks of pictures and her story. These ads will appear in selected newspapers and magazines. Ginger likes the word *selected*. Still, the idea of a tangible, filled-in image of herself seen by—what? who? thousands? millions?—terrifies her.

True to PoundSolve's word, smack in the middle of the next week the ads appear. Color! Full-page! Ginger opens a *Women's World*, and *oh, my god* there she *is! Is! Is!* Not *not-is*, not *is not!* And—Lord, Lord, Lord!—however they've done it, the fourth-week pictures scramble her weight and make her look even thinner.

When she goes to work the next morning, Thursday, Ginger waits for somebody at the firm to say something. When nobody does (instead asking her to take on yet another task), she flips, her hands shaking, through all the magazines in the waiting room, but none carry her image. Not *Time*, not *Newsweek*, not *Fortune*, not *Barron's*, not the *Wall Street Journal*, not even *GQ* or *Esquire*. So Ginger makes a note to herself to ask Clay and Waldo next time just what's on the list of *selective* magazines and newspapers?

But—on the street—people do recognize Ginger; people recognize her moving through the aisles of Smith's Food King. *It's her! It's her!* she hears. Strangers ask her how she feels. They ask whether she feels hungry all the time and what she plans to do with her new body and all her new money. Some people, though, especially thin women, silently speed their carts past her. Ginger senses their anger.

And then two or three days after the ads have first appeared one of those very thin women stops—her face purply-red—and confronts her. "No one's paying *me* any money!" she spits. "And I've looked like a knockout forever!"

• • •

By the middle of the sixth week, Ginger is office news—first with the stenos and go-fers, but very quickly with the junior partners and partners. She overhears the word *celebrity*! again and again—usually with admiration; once, though, with laughter. Then a junior partner named Keith Chapetto calls her into his office. "So!" he says—and grins.

Ginger briefly feels translucent, at least. Translucent again! Framed in Keith Chapetto's door, she can't construct an appropriate response to *So*!

Keith is still grinning. "So the news is out."

Ginger reaches for substance, for language.

"So—what have you lost so far?" Keith asks.

Eighty-seven pounds, she tells him.

He does the math on a yellow pad, blows air out in a half whistle. "Whoa! More than my salary," he says.

"But not for a lifetime," Ginger counters.

"*But not for a lifetime*. That's true; good point. Nevertheless!" He asks what her plans are for the money.

"Find a cure for cancer," Ginger says.

When he asks—then presses about—whether she has legal representation, Ginger excuses herself.

"So what's most different for you these days?" Keith Chapetto calls out after her.

• • •

What's most different? What's most different? Actually, it's a good question. Pinned to the wall, she would name three things: energy, will power, and tangibility. Number one, though, is clearly energy. Energy bursts inside her, daily, like firework grand finales. Instead of hunger pangs, she has energy bursts—bigger and bigger. And she has ever-again more fabulous ideas about what her life might become. The books she can write! The television series she can star in! The unsolved mysteries of science she can contribute to! The art gallery openings where people come and drink wine and eat tiny sandwiches and walk the space studying different variations on a theme that's *Ginger.*

. . .

She crosses the century mark of weight loss. Her nonnegotiable checks—now totaling $440,000—are given signatures by a man named Brian. Ginger can't make out the signature's last name; it looks like *Marsupial.* She's learned a thing or two as a legal assistant, and she puts all but $40,000 in various interest-bearing *instruments.* She likes using the word *instruments* in conversation.

Everywhere she goes she's recognized. She even starts to recognize her*self* and begins to feel herself on a bullet train—moving at high speeds from almost invisible to watercolor, then on to an amplified hologram, then a painting by Rubens, a Rodin sculpture, a guest on *Oprah.* "How's it going?" people on the street ask her. "How're you feeling?" She's a celebrity.

A question slips in and gradually becomes inflamed. "I'm just curious," she says to Clay and Waldo at their next shoot, "what's in this?" She shakes a quart-sized PoundSolve container.

"Mostly nucleic proteins," Clay offers.

"With methyl salicylate freeze-dried enzymes," Waldo adds.

"Everything is either organically grown or organically extracted," Clay finishes.

Another question strangers ask: "Are you doing this under a doctor's supervision?" It's a question that gathers increasing sense in its repeated asking, so she passes it on to her two benefactors.

Clay shrugs. He glances at Waldo. Waldo shrugs. What's to be said?

We have a company HMO," Waldo offers. "We could set something up. Checkup. Whatever. Be proactive. Run some lab stuff. Blood sugar. Thyroid. We could check your serotonin levels, put you on a treadmill and run a battery of stress stuff."

"Company expense."

Ginger says that the truth is she can't remember feeling better.

"Hey! If it ain't broke, don't fix it," Waldo jokes.

. . .

It's as though she's gone through a looking glass, Ginger thinks. In certain ways. She's never been here—never in this particular world. Always, in her memory, she's been overweight. Obese. Fat. There's a picture of her on her second birthday labeled *87 lbs*. In fact, she's never allowed herself to use the words *obese* or *fat* before, even in the deepest, saddest recesses of her mind.

So it's all discovery. She buys mirrors. She looks in them. She catches images of herself in glass storefronts, thrown back from the waxed fenders of cars. *Good Lord, oh, Lord! I'm beautiful!* She's lost 147 pounds. She weighs 165. She's been paid $588,000. None of the supermarkets or CVS drugstores can keep PoundSolve on the shelf. "You're a miracle!" both Clay and Waldo tell her almost daily.

Miracle, maybe, is the word, she thinks. It so stuns her that she's a person who's become *apparent* in the world—substantial, real, sometimes a hushed center of attraction. Again: she hasn't ever been here! In this world where a man named Tom Cruise is the March Hare! Where people who are named Paris Hilton and Kevin Bacon are the Walrus and the Carpenter.

As far back as Ginger can remember, she has lived only where bloatedness and unsatisfiable hunger lurk. In high school, the vocabulary words that haunted her were *balloon*, *distend*, *engorge*. The walls of any space always seemed too near. And if there had been any sexual awakenings, they'd scurried for the hollows and cracks and had submerged so as to not be recognized, lived hidden away like insects trapped under her skin, groundhogs burrowed deep inside her belly. So now, in a size 16 dress, everything is new and as powerful as a centerfold.

Each day brims with initiation. Her picture is everywhere; all the wire services carry her story. Ginger's not simply *copy*, she's *news*—thin, thinner, thinnest—and each day she is more and more beautiful and almost adolescently ripe. All the early-morning TV and radio talk shows want her! Clay and Waldo give her lists of appropriate and inappropriate topics to discuss when she's interviewed, acceptable and unacceptable answers. She memorizes them. She's bright. It's easy.

But it's the ordinary people who make her the most heady, women particularly. *You must be so incredibly strong! What is it now? Over 190 pounds? How are you ever going to spend all that money?* Still, once in a while, one is mean: *Have you any idea how hard you're making it for the rest of us?!*

When she hits the low 130s, three of the firm's lawyers start currying her favor. The first, Jacob, always takes her to restaurants he calls *bistros*, where he orders grilled snapper, drinks merlot, and talks about only two things: the stock market and professional football.

The second, Carl, always chooses Asian. He loves sushi; he adores Singapore noodles, pad thai, pho. Carl both scares and excites Ginger. He quizzes her about sexual fantasies, and she confesses that—truth told—she thought she'd never have sex. "But now anything's possible—right?" Carl asks, holding a round of shu mai on a fork, raising his eyebrows.

The third lawyer's name is Charles, and Charles is a fish maniac—a man obsessed with raw bars, places where he can peel shrimp and suck oysters. If he can get an ahi or mahi-mahi steak lightly seared, he's in heaven. Charles calls Ginger *Minnow* and is the first man ever to bed her, making her dizzy and breathless, tearful and confused. She's lost more than 170 pounds, and sexual sporting makes her lightheaded and unsteady. She thinks: *Shouldn't I be as much a part of this as he is? Shouldn't he be saying things like "I love you?"* Instead he just makes a lot of the same hunger-sounds he makes when they're together at the raw bar.

• • •

Alone in her new four-bedroom, gated-development house after an evening with Charles, Ginger stops in front of her full-length mirror and finds she's younger than she's ever thought of herself. She thinks: *I've just been born!* understanding the thought to be silly—giddy, girlish.

She rents several porn videos. They arouse her and she imagines herself starring in such a video where the woman—at the beginning of an hour of marathon sex—weighs more than 300 pounds and at the end weighs only 110. She could *write* that film. She could *star* in it. She would call the film *Ginger Does Ginger!* At 138, with nearly $700,000 banked, Ginger feels she can do anything. Say to Charles, *I don't want to see you anymore.* Say to the eager wannabe personal-manager-woman from New York, *Please don't call anymore.* Say to all the many others, calling to cash in: *Thank you, but no; I'm going to do it myself.*

She slips the last porno into its sleeve, takes a shower, touches herself, feels pleasure, washes her hair with almost brutal vigor, slips into a new terrycloth robe, descends the stairs to her kitchen, opens her fridge, stares in, smiles, closes it, climbs the carpeted stairs, and goes to bed.

• • •

Sometimes in her dreams, Ginger remains fat. Often the fat, sad Ginger asks, *Why won't you be my friend?*—her crying so crushing the new Ginger's breath that she wakes, twisting, gasping. One such morning—not fully understanding why—she plays the current week's all-network ad videotape. In it she weighs 122. She's wearing a dark shade of lip gloss and eyeliner. Her hair's been styled and curls in at her neck. Her wardrobe is Donna Karan—black with, here and there, red accessorizing. On the audio she says, "I've lost 180 pounds—and I feel *great*!" And then she runs her manicured nails up her bare arm and says, "Can you imagine what it feels like to—for the first time—realize you have *skin*? And that you skin's *alive*?"

• • •

At their next meeting Ginger asks Waldo and Clay point-blank, "When is it over?"

Clay and Waldo stare. It's as though she were the empty space on a rug from which a very expensive entertainment system has just been stolen.

"When do I stop?" she asks.

For an unnatural time, the room's only dialogue comes from the duct system and the wiring. A florescent buzzes overhead. A conditioning flange rattles. A grate whirs. A halogen bulb sounds anxious.

"I'm having trouble imagining myself thinner," Ginger says. "Yesterday—" Ginger tries to explain, "yesterday—I had this feeling that—I don't know—that I'd been walking down a long road, walking to meet myself. And…I had arrived. Does that make any—?"

"Jesus! Great line," Clay says.

"Write it down," Waldo says.

• • •

There are messages on Ginger's phone from Jacob, Carl, and Charles. *Is she free for dinner?* Other messages offer her product tie-ins, personal management, and media coverage. At first Ginger diligently returned all the calls from people and new people and newer people—all of them seeming as delicious and possible as a kind of *family*. Now she returns none. In only fourteen months, Ginger's world filled up—with everybody!—then emptied.

The last message is from Waldo. Is she free tonight? Maybe dinner. Everything would be unofficial, he says. Just dinner, just them, no obligations, no ties. No connection to product. No rules. Call him. He's serious.

Waldo, Ginger thinks. *Waldo. Dinner. No rules.* What's he talking about? What's he mean?

She calls. They agree. The restaurant Waldo names, Frisee, specializes in exotic salads, salads with goat cheese, chanterelle mushrooms, and vodka vinegars. When she arrives, Waldo is pacing by an aquarium. "Thank God! I thought you wouldn't *come,*" he says.

"Why?"

They sit and Waldo orders. (Why are these men always taking her to restaurants? Where there's food. It seems perverse.) Ginger thinks Waldo seems different without Clay—and says so.

"Well, hey, we're not the same person, you know," Waldo says. He takes a deep breath—one of many since Ginger's arrived and possibly before. "You've become very beautiful," he says, then adds: "I'm separated."

They go out for three nights in a row, kiss awkwardly once. Waldo has the mouth of a terrier, Ginger thinks.

Clay—in any of their work-related encounters—becomes edgy, silent, more watchful. At the next weighing and photographing, Clay steps in front of Waldo to walk Ginger to the elevator. "Something's going on," he observes.

Ginger studies his ears, his hair.

"Don't say 'I don't know what you're talking about' or 'Nothing.' Because I can sense—I have the ability to sense, you know, which I try not to abuse, but..." Clay's eyes become mean and sad. His pupils are the pupils of a snake in the oculus of a hound dog. "Okay, I'm not going to be coy, and I'm not going to freak out. Why him and not me?" Clay asks.

Ginger imagines then quickly rejects Clay as her sweating partner in the pornographic weight-loss movie.

Waldo calls early that evening and asks: What did Clay want? Why had he walked her to the elevator? But then he doesn't wait for her response. "He's a prick, you know!" he says—then immediately asks if he can come over.

Ginger invents a mother, a doting mother in Daytona Beach. It's her first lie since she started losing weight. "I would take better care of you than Clay," Waldo says before hanging up.

Ginger stands with her hand around the telephone shaft—as if it were a dog bone or a penis. Her eyelids drop like rolling metal warehouse doors. If there were liquor in her house, she thinks, she'd drink it. Like a movie alcoholic—gulp after desperate gulp—until she slid to the floor and passed out. But she hasn't stashed any liquor—only Almond Joys and bags of Lay's potato chips. She drops onto her couch, shuts her eyes, tries to reimagine the weight-loss porn video she'd imagined before—herself center stage and the object of inexhaustible hunger and lust. Strangely lit and shadowed protean images start to generate and move. *Someone* has his mouth on her breasts—she can almost smell the saliva. Then someone else has a gun in his hand. She's on an animal-skin rug. And—? Is she laughing or crying? Ginger reaches for and hugs a small pillow. Then she opens her eyes, rises, and goes to the kitchen sink. Over and over she splashes cold water on her face.

• • •

Ginger buys a three-way mirror, thinking that because she's now visible, when she stands in front of it she will have choices, a mix-and-match trio of Gingers. Instead, the glass alcove relentlessly and unequivocally says, *Ginger/Ginger/Ginger* to her again and again. What she sees is a young and beautiful woman—yes—yet undeniable shadows fly out in flocks—like bats or purple martins—from what must be caves in her skin, shadows all the colors of bruises. And there's a dim smell as well—of faint infection or overripe nectarines. Yes, she owns her life now, certainly; some kind of spell's been broken, Still, this is a world that aches—self-possession aside—and she's a part of it.

I need to do something, Ginger thinks. *Install a sauna. Something. Change banks*. A sudden idea strikes her. She wants some kind of release, climax, exorcism. Seeing the birdlike shadows dispersing from the shadows of her at the three-way mirror multiplies something—a question, a hope, a need.

She goes to her closet, opens it. She can see the Escada jacket, the Liberty scarf, the pistachio-colored knit of the St. John's dress, the Tiffany pearls. With one hand on the Wolford pantyhose, the other on the Ferragamo shoes, she begins to laugh. So many clothes have been given to her. So she mismatches herself—on purpose, subversively—and goes out to dinner, choosing a restaurant with the first name of its owner, *Warren's*, wondering whether the specialty dish there might not be rabbit.

Though she's not a whiskey drinker, Ginger starts with an old-fashioned.

"Maker's Mark or Jacob's Creek?" the waiter asks.

Ginger opts for the Jacob's Creek. She likes the sound the two words make—one against the other. Her old-fashioned arrives, and its first sip feels hot and meaty in her mouth, then throat, then belly, then beyond belly—deep inside. Something about herself-in-the-world has become delicious. The word *cannibal* glides like a snake through her brain. She becomes sexually lubricated, becomes aware that others in the restaurant have identified her.

"How's the Jacob's Creek?" the waiter stops by and asks.

"Exquisite," Ginger says, then smiles—because it's the first time she's used the word. "It tastes like a man's teeth."

Something snaps in her brain—something delicate and thin-boned, like a bird's wing.

The waiter lowers his head and angles away. Soon he's back, though, asking if she's ready to order. She says, no, no; she needs to read the menu; give her a minute. Then, with barely a syllable's pause, she says: "Actually—no; don't give me a minute; I've decided; I'll have one of each of the appetizers, one of each of the entrees, no desserts."

The waiter hovers, seems like kelp caught in an eddy or maybe a lodgepole pine in a windstorm. "It would seem I've misheard you," he finally says.

Ginger makes her order unequivocal. "Just spread them out over the table—bring them in any sequence; it doesn't matter."

"But—" the waiter begins, then—doing some quick math in his head—estimates what his tip will be on a bill of almost $3,000. "Yes, madam."

"I'll put it on a card," Ginger says. Then she smiles provocatively: "I can afford it," she says. And she hands the menu back to him.

She orders seven of the most expensive wines as well.

Now she has a staff of at least four devoted to her. The plates begin to arrive. There's goat cheese with snow peas and balsamic. There's scallop and fruit salsa. There's sashimi and blood orange. There's fettuccine alla burro dolce. There's bison and aromatic herbs in a reduction sauce. Ginger savors the delicious word *reduction*.

She takes one small bite from each offering, keeps it in her mouth like a long and deep kiss. With each—and with each tasting of wine—she registers appreciation or disinterest. Pretty soon, the man the restaurant is named after, Warren himself, is standing by her table. And others dining there—when Ginger smiles—are asking, "What was that wine she just tasted?" "What did she just sample?"

When she goes home she pleasures herself with a device that's been sent to her for an endorsement and sleeps in a way she's never slept before. In the morning the flowering plum trees in her yard stand out against the blue aquatic western sky with the high definition of an LED video screen. Ginger showers and, over a cup of espresso, reads about her night at Warren's in the morning paper. Someone took a picture, and there she is! Lovely! Unmistakable! More visible than hunger or poverty. More visible than Madonna or the vice president.

Within hours, men with names like Emeril and Wolfgang and Todd and Daniel are extending invitations to her—echoing one another and saying *please*. And *carte blanche! Carte blanche!* So she signs agreements and begins her life—leaving Waldo and Clay and the generous interests at PoundSolve gratefully, but necessarily, behind.

She signs agreements with men named André and Eric and Joel, makes appearances in their restaurants in New York, Miami, San Francisco, and Las Vegas, where she sits in the center of incredible decor and only samples, doesn't eat. Sometimes she takes a duck confit or Chambord reduction sauce between her fingers and sets just a dab of what she's squeezed in the hollow of her throat or behind her ears.

It's a life she's only imagined. And it's glorious.

My Life as a Thief

My life as a thief began at thirteen and was my father's fault. Or maybe it was Arthur Foley's father's. Fault, that is. Because he was a criminal—a man never at home, instead forever on the road and making—Arthur's word—*deals*. And then, later, not at home because he was locked up and—Arthur's words again—*pending trial*.

I asked Arthur what a *deal* was. He said: "I'm not sure. But it's big."

"Big!" Arthur's mother, Gin-gin-ginger, echoed from the next room, then moved into the frame—cigarette hanging from her thick lipstick, ashes scattering onto what she called her *housecoat* and into what she called her *toddy*. "No shit about it, Little Man," she said to Arthur. And then, "Big," she repeated—her word floating into the room and over our heads like a smoky balloon.

Arthur took me into their darkroom and showed me nude photos he'd taken of girls at Old Orchard Beach in Maine where they spent their summers. "Look!" he said; "You can see their pussies!" And he was right.

• • •

I started doing magic when I was eleven. It wasn't exactly my idea. My father, the doctor, brought me a half dozen tricks he'd bought at Jack & Jill's Novelty Shop, just off Washington Street in Boston. What he was doing there I don't know. His office was at Mass General, and Washington Street wasn't exactly his neighborhood. Also, it wasn't like him to think: *If my son's going to be any kind of magician, he'd better get a good start now.*

There were cups and balls. I remember that. And three decks of cards that you could do—the manual promised—a hundred tricks with. Easily. *Fool Your Friends. Amaze Your Relatives.* Maybe my father thought perusing the manual would increase my reading skills.

There was a wand that went limp—which was a kind of joke. You picked up the wand to make the card the person had chosen rise up from the deck, and at the magic moment the wand went limp. And the audience laughed. But you, the magician, had the last laugh. Because the card rose up from the deck anyway. And the wand straightened out.

Also, I remember, there was a finger guillotine. You'd put a carrot in it to show that the blade was sharp and knew its business and could de-digitalize someone. Then you asked for a volunteer. And you did all kinds of how-do-you-think-you'd-be-with-only-four-fingers jokes. And then you'd slam the blade down and leave the volunteer's finger intact but cut the little carrot in the small opening just below.

But I don't want this to be about rising cards or failed surgery. I want it to be about my life as a thief. It's just that it was magic that led me there. Magic was the path. Magic was the trail that led to my almost becoming a criminal—like Arthur Foley's father. To sitting in a cell with only bread and water, *pending trial.*

After I'd mastered the six tricks my doctor-father'd gotten for me, though, I was hooked. People paid attention when I performed. People thought I knew things they might never know. Secrets. What Arthur—who had also begun doing magic—called *mysterious shit.*

So I started taking the MTA to Washington Street and going over to Jack & Jill's. A man in a shiny blue suit demonstrated tricks for me, and I bought the ones I liked out of my allowance and some of the money I'd earned from selling homemade seashell jewelry around the neighborhood.

But Jack & Jill's was more about novelties and jokes than magic, and I was advised I might have better luck, broader selection, at Max Holden's over on Boylston. So, on a Saturday morning, I headed over there.

I remember that you had to take an elevator to get to Max Holden's. It was on the third floor. And I remember how excited I felt just in rising two floors. Because Max Holden's was a magic store. It was itself magical. I saw Thurston there one time! And Blackstone! All the great magicians went to Max Holden's when they were in Boston.

They hung out and showed one another variations they'd invented on the stock tricks. If you could make a canary appear, you could make a dove appear. If you could make a dove appear, you could make a hawk appear. If you could make a hawk appear, you could make a condor appear. And so on.

And if you could make something appear—you could also make it *dis*appear, make it vanish. And that's where my life as a thief comes in. There's a simple magic device, a small black cup attached to a cord of black elastic. You pin one end of the cord up your sleeve, stretch it *down* your sleeve, hold the cup in your hand, stuff a big floral silk handkerchief into your hand, thrust your hands forward, and—*magic!*—the silk is gone.

And I don't know why I didn't find this trick earlier in my magic career, but I didn't. Not until what my mother later called *the Arthur Foley era*. So now Arthur was with me; he was a magician too—a magician with a criminal father, which made a kind of sense. So we both bought this disappearing silk device on the same Saturday morning—after which we went to Jordan Marsh and rummaged around in the silk handkerchief department.

"Please put that silk back in the display," a clerk would say.

"What silk?" either Arthur or I would say and, in saying, thrust our hands forward. Empty. Clean.

"How—? But I just saw…"

And so it went. Jordan Marsh. Filene's. Town & Country.

Magic is the art of distraction. Crime as well.

By the end of a couple of hours we had at least $500 worth of expensive silk scarves between us.

A week later, we glued magnets inside our elastic-strung cups and—over two days between us—picked up twenty-eight (some of them Zippos and Duponts) cigarette lighters. Each of us had a trick called the Chafing Dish where you'd squirt lighter fluid into this silver dish, light it, cover it to put the fire out, lift the cover and-hey, presto—the dish would be filled with flowers. Or maybe a gerbil. Arthur had gerbils. Sad story: one died when we were doing the trick.

But the point…my point telling you this is: *How did it feel?* How did it feel to be a thief? It felt powerful! It felt great!

So that was it. My life as a thief began as magic. It was fun. Being a criminal was fun. We'd go into stores. Rummage around. Steal. (Arthur called it *lifting*.) And the clerks—all the clerks who thought they had us—were mystified.

But—as I guess with anything in life—the elastic-up-the-sleeve trick lost its...whatever: *rush*. We had done it...and done it. It had worked. The question of would-we-get-away-with-it-or-get-caught had been answered. We could steal Hermès scarves and cigarette lighters for the rest of our lives and no one would be the wiser.

So the challenge became: lose the cup and elastic and just steal. Walk into a store, any kind of store; it was—here's a vocabulary word for you—*arbitrary*, and steal.

We started at Berman's Pharmacy. At Max Holden's on Saturdays, we were getting lessons on palming—trapping something in your hand in a way that leaves your fingers out, extended, so that your hand, underneath, looks empty. So Arthur and I practiced palming at Berman's. We got aspirin. We got throat lozenges. We got cream with zinc in it. We got birth-control pills. Diuretics.

One time Mr. Berman came out from behind the counter and walked up to me. "Do you have something in your hand?" he asked. For some reason—I think it was the lab coat—when I heard the uncertainty in his voice, I pointed to an aisle of vitamins and said, "What is that vitamin in the red bottle?" And when he looked, I dropped and kicked the heisted condoms into the next aisle.

We had no use for the pharmacy stuff, so the question was: What should we do with it?

Arthur argued that we should throw it in the dumpster behind the First National. I argued that it was important to keep a record of our accomplishments—or *loot*—so we should think seriously about storage instead. When people fifty years from now did a study, they should have—another vocabulary word—an *archive*.

Arthur said, "Okay. What the fuck."

What the fuck. So: there was a gashed and dented trunk in our attic that my father, the doctor, had hauled home. From the war. And we stashed our pharmacy stuff there. Who knows: maybe the mice got high on the Sudafed or wild cherry cough syrup.

During our straight and magically unassisted shoplifting stretch, we took stuff from—besides Berman's Pharmacy—First National (mostly cans of crabmeat and packages of Lipton soup), Meister's Fish Market (smelts and oysters), Town & Country (panties and argyle socks), and Atwood's Art Supplies (tubes of burnt sienna and Chinese red). The smelts and oysters from Meister's Fish Market were a mistake. They were a challenge, and we liked the challenge, but we knew that we would regret it if we put them in the attic trunk with the condoms and the argyle socks.

We called the trunk the Trunk, as if it were a magic thing. An alive thing. Like a being/creature out of *Harry Potter* or *Lord of the Rings*. When we wanted to steal, we'd say, *The Trunk is hungry! We need to feed the Trunk!*

Stage 3 of my life as a thief was stealing from friends' houses. We stole silverware from Ned Bunyon's house. Forks! All wrapped up in a green cloth that was like a shoe-polishing cloth. Also a gold-colored ring that had stones in it. It was on the windowsill above the kitchen sink. I remember Ned saying that his mother never liked washing dishes with her rings on. At Ned's house we also got some kind of prescription medicine from the bathroom cabinet. And all those things we put in the Trunk.

"Feed me! Feed me!" Arthur Foley made up this funny monster voice. He was good at voices. "Feed me!"

We wondered if we should get a lock for the Trunk, but decided it wouldn't be necessary—it seemed it was a trunk no one in my house ever used or ever would.

Next was Rabbit McBride's house. Rabbit's family was Catholic and went to St. Joseph's. So there were a lot of Catholic things around. I don't know what they were; Rabbit had explained them, but I hadn't paid attention. Some were big, but where would we put those? But some were little—tiny statues, necklaces, something I remember Rabbit called a *scapular.* We stole a bunch of those. They were all around—easy to palm and then slip into our pockets or up our sleeves.

Also, Rabbit's father was what he called a *marksman*. He had guns. Some he'd brought home from the war. Rabbit said he and his dad went to the range almost every Saturday. So I said—on the day we stole the other stuff—to Rabbit: "Do you think you could show us your dad's guns again?" And he was happy to. It made him feel important, I think. One of the guns was a pistol—really small, really little. It was called a DoubleTap. And the whole gun was only, like, about three by five inches.

So I nodded to Arthur, who—being a magician—knew the art of distraction. And Arthur—in a kind of loud, barking voice—said, "Hey! What's that over there?!" And when Rabbit turned and looked over to where Arthur was pointing, I grabbed the DoubleTap from the drawer where it lay with some other pistols, shut the drawer, and said, "Hey! Let's go outside and play Frisbee!" Which we did for about twenty minutes until Arthur said—looking at his watch (which may, actually, have been a watch we'd stolen)—"Whoa! Sorry. I gotta get home. I promised my mom I'd go with her to my father's hearing."

"What's a hearing?" Rabbit asked.

"My mother says it's a long story," Arthur said. And we told Rabbit we'd see him around.

"Are there bullets in it?" Arthur asked as we were walking home.

"I don't know," I said.

"Point it somewhere. Shoot it!"

"What if there are?" I asked.

"We'll find out," he said. "Point it; shoot it."

"Later," I said.

Instead we put all the Catholic stuff and Rabbit McBride's mother's ring and even the DoubleTap in the Trunk.

"Feed me! Feed me!" Arthur broke up and started to laugh.

"I'm hungry! Feed me!" I repeated.

* * *

I don't want you to think that all Arthur Foley and I did during the whole ninth-grade year was steal from our friends' houses. I was a pretty good student; Arthur wasn't a bad one. So we had school. And then we did magic shows together at little kids' birthday parties. Somehow the word had spread that we were pretty good. A lot of Saturdays, then, we did shows. And of course we practiced. Magic's a skill. Stealing's a skill too. It's just, the point is, we didn't do it all the time. We did magic; we stole; we went to school, did our homework. We spaced the different things out.

Another friend's house we stole from—this one in the summer between ninth and tenth grade—was Felix Pardo's. Felix had come to the United States in the sixth grade from Madrid. In Spain. And he was a bit of a clown. But he was one amazing soccer player. And his house was a good house to be a thief in, because there were things everywhere. Objects! Funny, when I went there the first time and walked through the rooms, I said, "Look at all these things!" and Felix corrected me. He said, "*Objects.* My father says they're *objects.*" Felix's father, Felix said, was in the import-export business, and he was home even less than Arthur Foley's father, who actually was home quite a lot now because he was required, Arthur said, to go to hearings. "Something broke," Arthur said.

"What do you mean—*broke*?" I asked.

"Broke. Just broke," Arthur said. "My mother told me to mind my p's and q's and not ask about it."

Felix told us his father collected prints, and he took us into a small room that had a whole wall of cubbyholes. "My father had this room remodeled," Felix said, "for his prints." And he reached into a cubbyhole and pulled out a rolled paper. When he unrolled it we saw a color picture of a bearded man with a spear on a horse. Arthur and I nodded, and Felix rolled the picture back up and pulled out another. This one was just colors—blue and yellow and red. Then another with a woman floating over a house.

Some of the pictures were big, some small. I was wearing my windbreaker and sure I could stuff a small one up my sleeve. So I nodded to Arthur, who knew the nod and did a "What's this?!" pointing to the other side of the room. Distracting. And Arthur was really good; he could play a distraction like a violin, asking questions, dragging it out. While he did that, I started pulling different rolled pieces out. And when I found one only about eight inches long, I stuffed it up my sleeve.

When we got back to the Trunk, I unrolled it. It was just a drawing in ink: three acrobats on two trapezes. Someone had put their name on it, but it was hard to make it out. *T. Lautr...* Neither of us could read the end of it.

We put it in the Trunk.

On the Saturday before the Monday of the last week of school before summer break between our sophomore and junior years, I went over to Arthur's because I thought both our handcuff and our coin-pail tricks needed practice. Also I thought we needed to get more skillful with our spring and feather bouquet handling. Arthur's mother, Gin-gin-ginger, said he had gone with his father to Revere to *learn some secrets.*

"I'm just telling you what Connie said," Gin-gin-ginger told me. (Connie was Constantine Foley, Arthur's father.) "I'm just here by myself. You want to come in?"

I shrugged, walked in. Gin-gin-ginger closed the door.

"Want a drink?" Gin-gin-ginger asked. She was wearing dark jeans and a white T-shirt—no bra, I think, under it.

I nodded *yes.* I'd never really had a drink-drink. I'd watched my parents have wine with guests or a *nightcap* just before bed.

I watched Gin-gin-ginger pour something into a glass. "Ice?" she asked. "Neat? Do you want Coke or orange juice with this?"

"Orange juice," I said.

She poured orange juice in, handed over the glass, refilled the one she had. "Stars in your eyes!" she said and raised her drink.

"Right," I said, raising mine.

We drank.

"You're a nice-looking young man," Gin-gin-ginger said. "Arthur isn't. I've said. I've told him—it's not going to be your looks that grab a woman's attention. But he understands; there are other…I think the word is *incentives.* We've talked about that. Has he shown you his naked pussy collection? Some people say: You've seen one, you've seen them all, but those people have no idea what they're talking about…I'm glad you're here. I need company. They're not going to let Connie come up with us to Old Orchard; he has to stay within the state. So it will be just Arthur and me. Maybe you'd like to come up and spend a couple weeks. It's a great little Cape Cod—right on the beach. Well—almost. Almost on the beach. What do you think?"

"It's possible," I said.

"Yeah, right; everything is possible," Gin-gin-ginger said, and she downed her whole drink.

• • •

The summer came and went without crime. Almost. The first week after school let out and before I went away to Antrim, New Hampshire, to Sachem Boy Scout Camp to work kitchen staff, I took the MTA into Boston most days and went to Max Holden's and hung out with the magicians. I loved watching them share tricks. *But here's a twist on that!* one would say. And then they'd all lean in.

That same week—nights, after dinner—I'd go up to the attic and pull our stolen stuff out of the Trunk: silks, cigarette lighters, condoms, jewelry, the ink drawing of the acrobats, the DoubleTap. For some reason the DoubleTap confused me. Sometimes I'd just hold it for almost half an hour. One of those nights, as I was coming down the carpeted front stairs to say goodnight to my parents, I heard my father-the-doctor's voice raised (which was unusual): "I just wish he'd come close to his capacity!" To which I heard my mother reply, "Fred, he's a boy. Let him just be a boy."

So then I went off to scrub pots and peel potatoes and cut cabbage in the camp kitchen—where Harry, the drunk and insane cook, threw knives at me and locked me in the stand-up freezer for two hours. Which, I know, should give anyone nightmares, except—freed from the freezer—I could swim in the lake, and some nights we'd all walk into town and hang out with the local girls at Antrim Drugs.

Then it was first day of school junior year, and I tried to get Arthur to go out for football, but he said he had a sports allergy. And he was probably smart, because that same week I tore the ligament in my left knee and was on crutches for a month-plus. All of which cut down on the next stage of my life as a thief—but it swung back into full gear with Arthur about the second week in October, when—by a kind of unspoken understanding and, maybe, because Arthur confided that his father was going to have to serve time—we both knew we had to take our criminality to the next level.

What we decided upon was: breaking into houses. People who were out of town. Junior year we both had licenses, so we could drive around, comb neighborhoods. For a couple weeks I was still on crutches, and Arthur joked that I should be getting *thieves' disability*. We'd go by a house on a Monday. Write down the street and number. Go by on Tuesday—see if it checked out. Again on Wednesday.

Third week in October, we had a triple confirmation. Rule #1 was:

Nothing big. No exercise machines or microwaves or refrigerators. So we parked Arthur's car on Prentiss Lane, the street below the street where our targeted house was, and we went up a drive, crossed a back lawn, went through a hedge, and were in the backyard. We'd not thought beyond having an objective and arriving outside it. We had no lock-picking skills. Should we break a window? If we could get into the garage, could we get into the house?

In this case the answer was yes. The door to the garage in the back was kind of half-assed locked. After we'd jiggled the handle for a while, the door opened. And after that it was simple: the door from the garage to the house was unlocked, and we just (as my mother would say) *waltzed in.*

It was an interesting house. Neither of us knew the people. Their name, we saw from all the mail that had been dropped onto the floor from the mail slot, was Henderson. As far as we could figure the husband's name was Charles and the wife's Naomi. And there was another Henderson getting mail: Daphne.

We had flashlights. It would have been exciting to find a safe, and we looked all over for one—inside closets, behind pictures—but there wasn't one. Which was probably a good thing, because then we would have had to try to figure out how to open it. From the Hendersons' house we stole (even though we'd said *nothing big*) a Fender guitar. Arthur said that his mother—more than anything—wanted him to be in a band. So we stole the Fender, which even when we took it we knew we could never fit into the Trunk. Then we escaped the way we came and drove around for an hour or so.

Three days before our larceny at the Henderson house, I'd spent the whole afternoon at a Dr. Clovis's office—which was in his house, not far from our own. Dr. Clovis was a *psych*-something. *Therapist.* He gave me a bunch of tests. He'd say *gizzard*; I'd say *guts.* Stuff like that. He'd say a word; I'd pick a definition. He gave me puzzles—some with blocks and rings and other stuff. Get-the-lost-boy-out-of-the-maze was another thing we did. I was there from about 2:30 till after 6:00.

"How did you like Dr. Clovis?" My father, the doctor, asked at dinner.

"He was fine. He was all right, I guess," I said.

"He's a colleague of mine," my father said. And he smiled. He seemed happy.

Then, two days after we'd stolen the Fender guitar from the Hendersons', my father asked if we could talk. "Let's do it in your room," he said. *In my room? That* had never happened before, and the idea scared me. Still, I said yes.

I sat on my bed; my father sat at my desk chair. "I had a conversation," he said, "with Dr. Clovis this afternoon."

I just nodded.

"You scored very highly on the test," he said. "Extremely. Extremely highly," he added. And then: "Do you have...any sense of your ability?"

I shrugged. It wasn't a question I had an answer to.

"Do you not like school?" he asked.

"It's okay," I said.

"Why do you think it is that you don't do better?" my father asked. "Do you think just being above average is good enough?"

"I don't know," I said.

"I don't know either," he said. "In fact, it mystifies me—*has* mystified me—and then when I heard your scores..."

He said he had another colleague he would like me to see. "Talk to. He's in Cambridge. He'd like to start with just once a week. See how that goes. Would you be willing?"

"Sure," I said.

"I'm glad," my father said. "I'll give you the details. His office is easy to find. It's just off Harvard Square. He's a nice man. You'll like him."

• • •

Arthur's father was...I guess the word's *convicted*, and his going to prison for three to five years complicated Arthur's life. He was in and out of school, not available as much as before. Still, between October and the end of February, we were able to break into two more houses—homes where the families were on vacation or out of town. There were the Breeds, where we stole two pairs of Riedell figure skates. And the Hashimotos, where we stole a coin collection. Both (somewhere I learned the word) *plunders* were small enough to fit in the Trunk. The Hashimotos' coins caught my attention, so that I did some research and discovered that they weren't called coins; they were called tokens. And they were from an Australian Japanese internment camp during the war.

By March—St. Pat's Day—Arthur was back in school on a pretty regular basis. So we picked up doing magic together—visiting Holden's, doing kids' shows—and plotting our next move. I was glad he was back doing kind-of-normal things, but I could tell he was different. He was sad. And angry. One day he said, "I just want revenge."

The shrink my father'd asked me to see was nice. A nice man. I kept worrying he'd ask me about being a criminal. But he didn't. We just mostly (his word) *chatted*. "Tell me something you did that made you really feel smart," he'd say. And I'd skip over the silk scarves and talk about how I figured out a better way to peel carrots in the crazy cook's kitchen at Camp Sachem.

Something had just happened in Boston that Arthur and I talked a lot about. Three guys wearing overcoats and rubber Halloween masks had held up an armored truck.

"You dress like that—wear a mask—you could be *anybody*!" Arthur said. Somehow the idea made him come to life. I mean, like I'd never seen him before. He got excited, and we began riding the MTA in overcoats and rubber masks, sitting down next to people who were alone and in—I confess—creepy voices, striking up conversations. *Are you having a good day?* Not leaving the other person alone. *Oh—I'm getting off at that stop too! Are you hungry? Would you like to have lunch?* It was what I imagined acting in a play or movie would be like. I mean, because you were *you*—you know what I mean?—but *not*... but then again you *were*.

Arthur and I agreed: it was more exciting than being thieves. Much more. Don't ask us to explain. Someone later said we'd been street performers. It was just...you felt in charge; you felt powerful.

Well—powerful, yeah. Until...that's right—*until*.

It seems that in everything there's a next level. Freshman, sophomore, junior—like that. That was true of our being thieves, except even more. We kept needing to...raise the...roof, the rent. There's a word I can't...Be more on a kind of edge.

So after a month or so of our overcoat-and-mask MTA riding, Arthur had the idea that we should walk into a store—like, say, some department store—and just *move*, wander up and down the aisles. Hands in our pockets. So we picked the Harvard Co-op. It was right near the MTA bus and subway station.

So we did our bus thing—going into Cambridge. I had a Nixon mask; Arthur was a werewolf. *How're you doing? How's your day going?* That stuff. The thing was: when we sat down, we were pinning the other person by the window; they couldn't escape. So they just got more and more…scared, maybe, and uncomfortable, absolutely. *Please, don't talk to me*, the woman I was sitting beside said.

So we got to Harvard Square. Arthur was excited. "This is going to be amazing!" he said. And there was a weird tone in his voice that made me think he had something planned. "Wait till you see!" he said. It seemed like he had a plan. And then he said something I thought was really strange. He said, "Revenge!"

Okay, then. There was the co-op. Right across from us, next to Brigham's ice cream shop. So we waited for the light, crossed the street, turned to each other—Nixon and Werewolf—walked into the co-op, and started stalking the aisles.

Shoppers in the co-op were…I think *alarmed* is the right word. They moved to the side, kind of scattered. And then—I was only sort of half aware of this, but I could see Arthur pulling his right hand out of his overcoat pocket, and I was half aware that there was a gun in it—Rabbit McBride's father's DoubleTap. And then—from behind us—there were shots. And Arthur fell. And I froze. And three store detectives were there. And one threw me to the floor.

For some reason—stupid reason—it had never entered either of our heads that with our masks on no one could know that we were just kids.

But what had Arthur thought he would do with the DoubleTap? I still don't know.

They'd shot Arthur through the shoulder. An ambulance took him to Mount Auburn Hospital. He had some shattered bones, and he was there almost a week. I went over to his house to apologize to Gin-gin-ginger, and she gave me some scotch to drink. As we were drinking she started to cry and then said, "This is a fucked world. This is a fucked world we live in, you dumb little shit innocent." She said Arthur had been angry—*vengeful*, she said—about what *the system* had done to his father. And then what happened next was what she called *the sacrifice of the innocent*—she took me to her bed.

My father, the doctor, was upset about the co-op thing. "What gets into you?" he asked and then asked again: "What gets into you?" He told me he'd arranged for me to see Dr. Lymon, the shrink, twice a week. "What could you possibly have been thinking when you dressed up like that? *Did* that?"

I didn't have an answer. Or maybe I did have an answer, but I kept it to myself.

But—no question, no question about it—that was the end of my life as a thief.

Devouring Fire

An Interview

A Short History

I was born in Victor. Near Teton. Outside Driggs. In Idaho. On the way to Jackson Hole. Which most of you reading this have, I suspect, heard of. Jackson Hole.

It's a small town, Victor. Very. Off-season, most of the population could fit into the Knotty Pine for some BBQ and an evening of Fins and Fiddles, our local bluegrass group. I grew up and went to school there—Victor—K through 12—doing normal things, usual things: church, scouting. I was a guard in basketball and I pitched. Baseball. I had one of the leads in the senior play. I played a clumsy detective. Type casting. I also edited the school paper.

Summer of senior year I worked as a fishing guide for Ricky's Rafting River Trips. There were excellent hatches in the morning, so we put in on the Teton at 7:00 and floated till 10. It was all catch and release. I tied flies and was partial, I confess, to hoppers and humpies. When a client's fly got struck, I netted the fish. Slid them back into the current. Which made me, each time, feel like a priest absolving a sinner. Which was spooky. But cool. It was a small raft—Ricky's raft—with a two-customer max. Most clients were nice and tipped. Of course there were jerks. But you expect that. Doctors. Surgeons. People who hold other people's lives in their hands and feel superior. I won't go into detail, but trust me—jerks.

There was one girl client—Cora—about my age. And I know I shouldn't've, but I couldn't stop watching her. Still: I was careful; I stayed distant. I didn't let myself get heated up. I had been told I was a good employee, and why mess with that?

After graduation I attended Idaho State. In Pocatello. I majored in journalism and communications. Or communications and journalism. Depends on who asks: *What'd you major in?* I'd been the editor of my school newspaper. I said that. I liked interviewing. People. It was sort of like archeology: you dig, and—if you dig carefully—you find stuff. And sometimes the stuff's amazing. It made me feel I was a person with an intention. Interviewing. Eager. Someone with an itch. A confusing-at-times kind of curiosity. Which was true. Because that's pretty much me: confused but curious. Or curious but confused.

I did well at Idaho State. Seriously. The professors liked me. Even the semi-famous ones. I was assistant editor of the *Bengal* and graduated cum laude. After college I worked in the newsroom of the *Idaho Statesman*. My father said, "Well—you're either lucky or good." That was five years ago, and I've moved from small stories to bigger ones, and I've even begun to place pieces in magazines like *Runner's World* and *Colorado Runner.*

I also landed a piece in *Outside Magazine* on Craters of the Moon. National Monument & Preserve. It was called "Camping over in a Nightmare," and the title—I'm not kidding—said it all. Way back when, the Shoshones moved across where I was—moving from the Snake River to their encampments. I read a Shoshone legend about a huge snake—or *serpent* is what the book called it—a huge *serpent* on a mountain—who got angry at the lightning and coiled around and squeezed the mountain until lava shot from the openings and the mountain exploded. I thought I saw a little bit of that the night I camped there: snakes and fire. Ground exploding. Sometimes a person's mind can be a stranger. A dark stranger.

Some of that, I think, crept into my article. Because—though it wasn't my intention—the piece read like *National Geographic* meets *Nightmare on Elm Street.* A lot of hits. Lot of responses. Sandy Rickman, my *Outside* editor, emailed me: "I like what you do because it's dangerous." *Dangerous*! Hey: I'm a kid from Victor, Idaho—*dangerous*! Sandy Rickman said, "I sometimes dream that I'm being burned alive, and that's what the best of your writing is like: like I'm at the edge of ashes." *Edge of ashes*—Jesus, c'mon! Still, it led—two months later—to an interview with the famous fire and glass eater Anthony Aquilla.

Prelude

Anthony Aquilla was eighty-nine when I interviewed him. I had seen tapes. Him performing. And even though they were just tapes—and here's *dangerous* again—I'd had the feeling: *Be careful. Careful* (1) because it was hard to believe—I mean the amount of glass and fire he ate—the *magnitude*; and *careful* (2) because of the hours he kept at it—the *longitude*. This was killer stuff—the glass, the fire—and he *consumed* it. *Devoured*. Chewed and inhaled. Swallowed and digested. Then, with a black cup-measuring scoop—he leaned into the flames and ate more.

I'll confess here: I was drawn to his image. It was like one I'd seen in my History of Religions course at State; he was an *ascetic*. A kind of harp with skin. Bare feet. Ribs like a rack of lamb. Deep hollow *cavernous* eyes. You could almost hear his eyes echo. Shabby, torn clothes. I got the sense that whatever he did, at the same time he could stand back and watch himself doing it. You could imagine him…overseeing some kind of fire-and-glass-eating factory inside himself, checking the assembly line—the conveyer belts taking the fire-and-glass into a processing room, where it was chemically sprayed, then sorted. His tapes presented him as some kind of mystic-mechanic and I—I don't quite, specifically, know how to say it—and I…I guess the right word is *witnessed*: I *witnessed* it.

Again: the feeling of…*if you go there and interview this guy, be careful.*

One tape had a long fire section that began with a black and blurred screen. Followed by music. Then Aquilla's image. constructing slowly. Resolving. Himself circled by bundles of dry tinder. Which he'd light. Then allow to build. Into a blaze. Then finally, he would—I mean, it was right there on tape!—*inhale* until all the flames had disappeared and he stood—chest out—filled with fire. I mean, you could *see* it. Seriously! Him *tasting* the flames. Rolling them around in his mouth. Feeling their *legs* in his throat. Like wine. Finding their *nose* in his flared nostrils. Then he'd swallow.

I mean: *Jesus Christ, how does a person do this? Where do the flames go?*

I thought, *When I do this interview I can't cross certain lines.* But what the lines were I didn't know. I almost called *Outside* to suggest they had the wrong writer. But then I figured *Whatever happens, I'll learn something.*

And I did.

• • •

I called Mr. Aquilla in early April. He was at his home in Parowan, Utah. Over the phone his voice sounded granular. Like scree—but also assured. It was not the voice of an aging man. It was confident. Diffident. Like two voices in one voice. Also it was something else: tired, urgent, disappointed.

I explained I'd spent time watching his film footage.

He said, "I am not my filmography."

I said, "I know. I understand."

He said, "I'm not sure you do."

I apologized. For what, I don't know; who can say? Whatever. I apologized. It's a thing I do.

He laughed a gravelly laugh and said, "Send me your credits." He meant other interviews. I'd done two and agreed. I asked for his email.

"I don't use email," he said.

I apologized. Again. Said I was sorry.

"For what?" he asked.

I said no problem; I'd send him the interviews.

He said: "This is not a good beginning."

The call ended, but *not a good beginning* hung in the air. I'm an amiable person. I've been brought up that way. Over three summers, guiding for Ricky's Rafting River Trips—from the putting-in to the taking-out—it was always amiable. Pleasant. But there was something about Anthony Aquilla's voice and words that warned me (again): *Be careful.* Gaining his trust wasn't going to be easy.

I reran the footage—him standing in his circle of fires. I looked hard, studied the flames, saw them flicker and flare up. Like a prayer, almost, to the night sky. Then I watched the leaping blades of heat suddenly right-angle and travel like arrows into his lungs. He was inhaling beyond inhalation. And I thought: *Jesus Christ, surely this is some trick, some deception, some fabrication*, but the footage seemed raw, appeared to have been taken with a handheld camera in real time. Without editing.

What I wondered was: *What's inside a man who eats glass and fire?* Does he have a different hunger than *my* hunger...which is, basically: do as much as you can in any day so as not to be *blamed* for anything.

I sent him both my interviews—one with a dance department choreographer I wrote for the *Bengal*, the other with a U.S. senator that was published in the *Idaho Statesman*. Also I sent my *Outside* piece.

He wrote back that I'd asked, he thought, good questions. But he said my writing had no *voice* and asked why I thought that was. He agreed to have me come and requested that I call him.

When I called, he suggested a first visit in late September. "I have California to deal with in the meantime," he said.

"California?" I asked.

"Walk outside," he said. "Lift your head. Up. High. Smell the air. Wet your hands; hold them up."

"Oh," I said.

"Oh," he said. "The black spots on your palms are not bugs."

"I get it: ashes. The fires," I said.

"I don't think you *do* get it," he said. "But right—yes—*the fires*."

The Plan

I would be traveling to Utah from Connecticut, where I guest-taught an undergraduate journalism course at the University of Bridgeport, an institution built on the estate of P. T. Barnum. I'd fly from Hartford/Springfield to Salt Lake, rent a car, and drive south.

"How will I recognize you?" Aquilla asked.

"Will there be others coming?" I said.

"I draw a crowd," he said—then laughed and went on, "I'm amusing myself. There'll just be the two of us. Still, my question remains. Imagine it still hanging in the air: *How will I recognize you?* What's your answer?"

"I'll be—I don't know—the bearded and almost balding guy," I tried, "with the red carnation in the lapel of my corduroy jacket."

"Don't attempt to be funny," he said. "How will I recognize you?"

"I'll be genuinely curious," I said.

"Why do I see you as genuine but incurious?" Aquilla said.

"Maybe I'll be curiously genuine," I said.

Aquilla laughed. "Good. Better. Much better," he mused.

Our Meeting—September, Two Years Ago

Mr. Aquilla lived off the grid in a hexagonal log home at the end of an unimproved road on a hillside roughly seven miles from the village of Parowan. It took time to find him. The rental car's GPS seemed indecisive and confused: was the turn onto his property a county road or a driveway? It kept passing his RFD mailbox and then running a loop of *Recalculating.*

On the way up the incline to his home, I drove cautiously, because there were goats and sheep milling. I could see what I took to be a sheepherder's wagon in the distance. And there were huge boulders—some of which had necessitated the road's redesign. Finally Aquilla's small home appeared—rough but tidy. He was outside sorting pieces of broken glass into different-colored bins. I've described him earlier. In the present moment, he seemed all that I've said amplified. He did not look like a man in his late eighties.

I pulled into a clear area, got out, and introduced myself. He gave me a quick study and nodded. "I'd take your hand," he said, "but I might cut you. My own has considerable glass embedded in it." He showed me, then asked, "Where's the carnation in your lapel? How do I know you're you?"

I stuttered, but he just threw his head back and laughed. Then he held his hand out to shake. His hand was like a mosaic dish.

"I would think you'd bleed," I said.

"I do," he said. "Just not at the moment."

"I'm sorry I'm late," I said.

"Are you?" he said. He checked his wrist. He wasn't wearing a watch.

"We'd said 4:00," I said.

"I think *you'd* said 4:00," he said.

"Possibly," I said.

Mr. Aquilla suggested we go inside. Find a couple of chairs. Bring them out where we could enjoy the late afternoon. "And begin this," he said. "My 'interview.'" He laughed again.

I remarked on how clear the local air seemed.

"This valley funnels and purifies," he said. "That's why I built here. The air's a river when it comes through. A sometimes swift, sometimes drifting river. And there's no one to throw beer cans or strangling plastic into it."

"You have—" I nodded toward the cabin, "—electricity." For whatever reason, I was surprised.

"*Me? I* have electricity?" Anthony Aquilla asked.

"I meant your cabin, your property."

"Well—all considered—I *am* my property," he said. Smiled. "Am I not?" He scooped some half-empty Coors bottles, crushed them in his fists. "Sit," he said. He threw the crushed Coors into the amber bin. "I'll get us something to drink," he said and went back inside. He returned with two whiskey glasses filled with ice. And a jug. "On special occasions I drink," he said. "I think Mondays are special occasions. Of course, today is Tuesday. But Tuesday sits beside Monday. So—might you join me?"

I said yes, and he filled two glasses almost to the brim. "You tied flies?" he said. "Onto the lines of strangers?"

"I did," I said. "For three summers. I—"

"What's the difference between an Adams and a Parachute Adams?" he asked.

"Well, a Parachute—"

"What's the difference between an Elk-Hair Caddis and a Blue Caddis?"

"Is there a Blue Caddis?"

"I don't know. I'm just trying to plant certain things in our conversation."

"Might we, instead, talk about—" I tried shifting the conversation.

"We might. Women?" he asked. And laughed.

"Whoa!" I had just taken a drink. "I mean, what *is* this? What you poured?"

"I distill," he said.

"Yes, I see," I said. "And the taste. What?" I asked.

"What's the difference between a Red and an Orange Humpy?" He laughed again.

I swirled the liquid in my glass. Made what I guess you'd call *an effort* to catch my breath.

"It's a secret," he said. Again laughed. "Bottoms up," he said. "To the world of Gypsies!" he said. He raised his glass. "To all those who are magical and unrooted!" And then drained it.

I drank. More...I think the word is: *judiciously.* Whatever the distillate, it was sweet. And rich. And strong. My head swam. "You distill well," I said.

"It's an old and very secret formula," he said, "which will die with me."

"I don't want to abuse your generosity," I said.

"Why not? You already have," he said. And again he laughed. He was laughing a lot. But he was not being what I would call *jolly.*

"Should we begin?" I said. I worried that, thanks to whatever it was that he'd distilled, I wouldn't stay clear.

"Here I am," Anthony Aquilla said. Which was true. He was. *Here.* There. At an angle in front of me.

"Okay." I checked my notes. I felt it best that I get seriously into the interview before the drink took effect. "When you perform—" I began.

"Ho! No-no-no-no. I don't *perform.* Bad way to start. I'm in no way a *performer.*"

"Sorry. Then, well...what is it you would call what you do?"

"Ingestion."

"In-*ges*tion?"

"Ingestion."

"You ingest."

"I ingest glass and fire."

"Because? Toward what end?"

"Enlightenment."

The word he'd used, *enlightenment,* positioned itself like a Sumo wrestler in a ring. It seemed territorial, immovable, strange. I tried approaching him from another side.

"Who taught you your craft?" I asked.

"What's the difference between a Pale Evening Dun and a Burnt Wing Pale Evening Dun?" he said.

"Who taught you your craft?"

"I traveled."

"And—?"

"Observed."

"Where? Your travel?"

"China. India. I don't think this is going well. Do you?"

"Sir, I don't mean to be troublesome, but—"

"Be troublesome."

"You're the one who keeps changing the conversation."

"You seem to be a young man who needs to be more troublesome. So you'd agree that this has not started well."

"Did I—I don't know—jump into…whatever—*craft* too fast?"

"You call it *craft*?"

"Well—"

"Why do you call it *craft*?"

I flared somewhat. I didn't mean to but I did. "You rehearse an art!" I snapped. "You paid attention and learned from others. Tricks and ways. You've learned the elegance and grace of those who've come before. That, to me, is *craft*. Why *not* call it *craft*? What it was you learned. Who it was that you learned from. What would *you* call it?"

Mr. Aquilla stood up and walked away from me. I felt bad. He moved to his different-colored bins, reached into the red one, filled his fist with shards, crushed them, dribbled the glass into his mouth, moved it around, swallowed it, sat down again.

"I asked a question," I said finally. "I asked what you would call—"

"I would call it, probably, *what I do*," he said.

"Okay."

"*Who I am*."

"Okay. Fine."

"Do you not believe that any person is the sum total of his doing?" Aquilla asked.

"Which makes you who? What? The World's Greatest Eater of Fire and Glass?"

"What's the difference between a Cripple Callibaetis and a Daddy Long-Legs Crane Fly?"

"Stop doing that! Okay?! Please?!"

The air—amniotic as it already was—set into a kind of gelatin. Insects found themselves trapped in it. As in amber. Birds struggled to escape. I had never, in my entire life, raised my voice like I had just done.

Anthony Aquilla rose from his chair. The sun moved more quickly now—lower and then lower in the sky. He drained his glass and then stared—harder and then harder still—at the horizon.

I was about to apologize when he turned back.

"I ate almost all of California this summer," he said. "Do you know what that says? About us? About how much fire there'll be in another year? Next year it will be Washington State. Then Oregon. Five years from now I'll be eating Travis City, Michigan. Peoria. Have you ever seen glass melt? Little ponds and estuaries in the cracked earth and dust? What's the difference between a—? Never mind; don't answer it; it's a trick question. Have I been rude? Don't pause; the answer's *yes*. So—!" And he began walking back toward his chair. "India and China: did I have teachers? I had *spiritual advisors*. What gets printed—about India and China—is misinformation. The impression, often, is of impoverished and constricted people. Defeated and malnourished. Stooped and bound. Untrue! Untrue. Those from whom I learned and with whom I remain friends are almost shockingly *un*bound. They are people who dream themselves forward. Here—in this country—you hear idle talk: *I put one foot after another*. Where I traveled—and with those from whom I've learned—the task is never *one foot after another*; rather, *one dream after another*."

I waited during a long silence. "There's not much information," I finally said. "About you. I mean, on the Web. Out there."

"*Out* there?"

"I thought you would have a Wikipedia entry. Well, actually you *do*; you *have* one, but it just says 'Fabled Midway Performer.'"

"Between what?"

"I don't . . . I don't think I—"

"Midway between *what*?"

"Oh, right. I see; I get it. But seriously, not much in the way of coverage. Of background. Mostly it's from people who have seen you. *Reviewers*, whatever you'd call them."

"How about we call them *journalists*? Like yourself. Are you a journalist? Do you *see* yourself as a journalist?"

"I—"

"Do you *see* yourself?"

"I haven't, exactly—"

"*I* see you. And I'll tell you: you're a *guide*. You're a *nascent* guide." He laughed.

Guided Imagery

"You're a guide."

"Well...once. For a while. Summers. True, I did—, I was—, but—"

"You're a *guide*. And if you're a guide—which you were and can be again—you never stop *being* a guide. Why would you do that? Stop? Delivering people to where they want to go?"

"Well, I mean...I went away. That's what ended it; I went away. To college, I guess. I graduated."

"From what?"

"You're confusing me."

"It's intentional. I am not a *story*. It's important to understand that. And that the time you spend—here, with me, is as a Guide and not a Journalist. Oh, I've been approached by journalists over the years—when I was 'within reach' I've been contacted. Contacted by people looking for a story. Which I'm not. I'm a *koan*. I'm a collection of koans. Written on rice paper. Do you know koans? Any idea what a koan is?"

"A poem?"

"Well, yes. On occasion. What would be the occasion? What sort?"

"Mystical?"

"A man traveling across a field encountered a tiger. He fled—the tiger after him. Coming to a precipice, he caught hold of the root of a wild vine and swung himself down over the edge. The tiger growled at him from above. Trembling, the man looked down to where, far below, another tiger was waiting to eat him. Only the vine sustained him. Two mice, one white and one black, little by little started to gnaw away the vine. The man saw a luscious strawberry near him. Still grasping the vine with one hand, he plucked the strawberry with the other. How sweet it tasted!"

"So...okay: doomed above and below—right?—he tastes the moment. Close?"

"Don't guess, please. This is not a guessing game."

"Except you set it up that way. Listen, I'm sorry; I don't mean to be argumentative. I know you don't usually do this—"

"Lad—"

"Robbie."

"*Robbie.*"

"With *two b*'s."

"Robbie."

"Right."

"I *never* do this. Meet with anyone who might be seeing me as a story."

"So... right. I mean, I'm thankful, grateful. Back, though—can we go back? if it's okay—to India and China? You went there—right?—*to be taught.*"

"To be *guided.*"

"Right. To accrue—is *accrue* a word? I think so; never mind: *study*. Okay. So I'm assuming that there is—right?—a tradition there. Of what you do. Glass and fire eating?"

"There is a body—are you familiar with bodies?—an ancient body of *knowledge*. One is initiated. One seeks and, seeking, experiences initiation. In America I have seen what I would call *pay-your-money-and-get-your-ticket*. But in China/India—with the Old Ones like myself now; I am an Old One—that is not the way. It may happen. Or may not. You do not find the Old One; the Old One finds you."

"And you went—?"

"And was found. Yes. As you have been."

"As I—?"

"*Found.*"

"And were taught secrets."

"Secrets were revealed."

"Right. So—weird; my head feels light, I think. Probably the—" I raised my glass. Anthony Aquilla filled it. "So... at what age—once back here, back in the United States—was it that you started to perform? Whoops! Sorry. Wrong! You don't perform."

"I *search.*"

"You search."

"As you will. *Search* and *explore.*"

"Okay."

"*Reach.* Do you understand *reach*?"

"I think—"

"Reach and eat glass. Swallow fire. When I went to China and India the first year, when I was in Jiangxi Province, I was imprisoned."

"For—?"

"They said: *Gathering a crowd.*"

"*Gathering a crowd?*"

"Yes."

"Because—? I mean, because you were...?"

"Preparing myself."

"For—?"

"You will see. You will begin. This evening, with me. I will guide the guide. You will begin your journey into the Life of the Dragon! It's an exercise—involving tree roots and pyracantha. And glass. And fire. You build a temple. If you do it properly, it will ignite itself. You empty your mind. And then you breath the fire into yourself...out of yourself. Crush glass; ingest glass. And then again. And again. The Life of the Dragon! It's a basic discipline."

"I'll take notes."

"No! No-no-no-no-no! No. No notes. None. No. You will *enter.* You will *begin.*"

Mr. Aquilla was there, and then he was gone. He disappeared into his house. There was a series of sounds like the breaking of branches followed by the puffing of a bellows. Then, with the same suddenness that he had entered his house, he exited. In one hand he carried an animal-skin bag at the end of a stick. Puffs of what looked like dust filtered out of it. He began rummaging in several of his glass bins.

"Breathe deeply!" he called over. "Breathe as deeply as you can deeply breathe."

I thought: *What are my choices? I'm being given an Anthony Aquilla firsthand demonstration. Is there any better kind of interview?*

Mr. Aquilla inspected what he had in his hands, what he'd taken from the bins. He nodded to himself. He seemed satisfied.

I was breathing deeply—or trying to. He approached. "Are you right-handed or left?" he asked.

"Left," I said.

"Hold out your right hand," he said.

I held out my right hand.

"Are you breathing slowly?"

"Sort of," I said.

"Okay," he said. And then he started placing pinches of what looked like dry bark and twigs into my palm, pressing them, compacting them there. "Don't move," he said. I could feel the weight of his breath on my hands, breath that smelled like ashes. He strode back toward the near outside wall of his house to where what I'd presumed to be an outdoor cooking fire sent a very thin scarf of smoke into the air.

He leaned down. Rummaged. Found a thin, dry stick, set it in where the scarf of smoke rose. There were tiny popping sounds. It lit. He turned and again walked toward me—his breath streaming in a steady current toward the end of the stick. When he was near he said, "When I light what's in your hand, close your hand slowly. And by *slowly*, I mean *s-l-o-w-l-y*. There will be fire there. You will experience fire. And remember: everything is in the hands. It all begins in the hands."

He lit the tinder. I could feel it burn. I curled the tips of my fingers toward the palm of my hand.

"*S-l-o-w-l-y!*" He elongated the word so much it sounded like slow motion.

I started closing my hand. It was on fire—ablaze—or I thought.

"Say to yourself: *I am not burning... I am not burning*," Mr. Aquilla said.

"I am not burning... I am not burning."

My hand was half open now—or half closed—and, though the flame in it leapt larger, any feeling of burning stopped.

"I am not burning... I am not burning."

My hand closed. A kind of oily smoke seeped between my fingers.

"Very slowly—subtly—have your hand massage itself." He demonstrated.

I tried that. He kept demonstrating. I got the knack.

"Now move your hand to your mouth. Tip your head back. *Tip your head back!* Open your hand and eat the fire. Eat what's in it."

I did as he instructed.

"Swallow."

I swallowed.

"Good," he said. "Good. How do you feel?"

Something like a sky of distant sheet lightning I'd seen once on the Teton River at dusk flared across the back of my brain. "Like I've been doing shots," I said.

"You have," he said. And laughed. Then laughed louder. "Doing shots," he repeated to himself and laughed again. "Okay!" he said. "First the fire—then the glass. Most people assume that the fire is harder than the glass—I mean I ate almost 70 percent of California last summer—but in fact the glass is more difficult."

"I would have guessed—"

"Hold both hands out this time."

I did. My right hand had some sketchy char marks on it.

"Okay: I'm going to give you two kinds of glass. Broken glass—glass fragments. The fragments I'll put into your left hand are from a Bombay Sapphire bottle. They're blue. The fragments I'll put into your right are from a Galliano bottle. They're yellow. Here. Look. Understand?"

"Yes, sir."

"You're sure?"

"I guess."

"No-no-no. No; don't guess. This is important. Do you understand what it is I'm telling you? About the origins and the colors of the glass?"

"Yes, sir."

"Good. Now—" He indicated what I should do next. "Please."

I cupped my hands. He slid the broken blue glass shards into my left hand, the yellow into my right.

"Are you able to close your fingers over the pieces that I've poured there?"

"Just barely," I said.

"That's perfect. That will work," he said. And then: "Okay. Shut your eyes. You needn't clamp them; just shut them. Shut them."

I did.

"Good. Now, as you did with the fire, breathe deeply. Deeply. Try...this will most likely sound more difficult than it is. Try thinking of yourself—try *imagining* yourself—as only breath. As simply a *being*, just a *presence* of breath."

I attempted that.

"Okay, good. Now cup your hands together so that they form a bowl. A ball, a sphere—fingers slightly interlocked... Good, that's right; that's excellent."

I could feel the sharp edges of the glass. Like thorns. Like little knife blades.

"Good... good," Mr. Aquilla said. "Good. Now—slowly—squeeze. Bring your palms together. But—! But before you do that, I want you to chant this to yourself. Quietly. What's important is that you *say* it and not that I hear it. And what I want you to chant is: *I am impenetrable... I am impenetrable... I am impenetrable.*"

"I..."

"Right! Yes!"

"... am impenetrable."

"Good! Now hold your hands above your head."

I did. "I am..."

"And start squeezing. Keep your eyes closed."

"... impenetrable." I could feel something running down my wrists.

"Hands together—press them—so that the palms touch."

Something hot, sticky. "I am impenetrable," I said.

"Believe what you're saying. Crush the glass."

Even—just whisper-chanting—my words were dry words. From a dry throat. "I am..."

"Crush it. Talk to it; let it talk to you. At first it will become fire-glass. And then glitter."

One time in Driggs I saw an auto mechanic changing a car's oil.

"Okay: enough... enough."

The engine oil ran down his arms just like—

"Enough, lad!" Mr. Aquilla said.

I wasn't sure what I was supposed to do next.

"Breathe deeply again—in and out. Slowly open your eyes. Slowly."

Which I did—expecting to see my arms soaked in blood, my hands torn open. Instead what I saw seemed like an oily fountain of sweat. "I'm not cut," I said.

"No," Anthony Aquilla said. "No, Robbie. Your skin—run your fingers over it—your skin's a little raw, a little ragged. It will take a while. But you were good; you managed the critical; you stayed with it; you believed—mostly believed—what you said. That you were impenetrable. Look what you have," he said.

Resting in my left hand was an opaque, slightly curled, flattened piece of glass the color of a Tanqueray bottle, only muddier. Like beach glass, only murkier. But there was no question that the yellow and blue glass I'd squeezed had spawned this result.

The sky lit. Shimmered. Dimmed. "Is there any more of what was in that jug?" I asked.

"Help yourself," Anthony Aquilla said.

I did. "So—"

"Just breathe. Just move ever so slowly. Quiet yourself."

I did. I drank the liquor and poured a little more. Tried to do what Mr. Aquilla had asked. Quiet myself. But it was like I was in a video game: a lot of flashes, explosions—all of which were questions. "So…just for studying with the people you studied with you were imprisoned?"

"Yes. Because a crowd gathered. But you can relax. There's no crowd here."

"How long? I'm sorry, I mean your imprisonment."

"A while."

"How long?"

"You learn thoughtfully. You learn well. Twenty-three years."

"That's…wow, yeah, that's a *while*."

"I've been told that."

"Were you—I mean, where you were, in your cell—deprived of—?"

"Water. Light. Warmth. Yes. I was."

"And was—?"

"What?"

"I don't know: survival—?"

"What?"

"I don't know. I'm—I don't even know what I'm asking."

"I stole glass. I broke it. Ate it. Used a small rounded piece as magnifier. In the morning sunlight came through a…break, a slit—not really a window. I used the magnifier to ignite my clothes and ate the fire."

"Did doing that—eating the glass and fire…I don't know, make you—I don't know how it could, but—you know, did it make you *stronger*? I'm looking for a word. There's a word; I can't think of it. Oh. Did it *fortify* you? And when there was no more, when there was no longer fire and glass, what did you eat then?"

"You just spoke of what I ate then." He laughed.

"What?"

"Words. I ate words. I slipped ceramic bowls of them into my cell. Verbs! I loved the verbs. Nouns too, but nouns are deceptive. They look robust, but in fact they have fewer calories. You lose them. Some adjectives, a few adverbs. Here and there a conjunction. An article."

"And what would they…I guess, *taste* like? The words?" I guessed: "Chrysanthemums? Pebbles from a streambed?"

"Bugs. Insect larvae. Fish minnows. When I ate glass, I gained focus. It gave me balance. Balance is life. I can ropewalk. Ropewalking is not for an acrophobic, but it is much simpler and easier than you'd imagine."

"So you returned here? To this country. To where you are now. Where *we* are. *Here*. How long have you been here?"

"A while."

"I read you've done this—what you do—for close to sixty years now. True? I mean, if you look at it a certain way, you're a pioneer. A 'settler,' one of the articles said."

"When you had the glass in your hands, when you crushed it—could you *taste* it? On the roof of your mouth? On your tongue? In your throat?"

"I could. I think I could. I think so."

"Yes?"

"Yes. You're—I'm sure you know—a legend. I mean not just here—Parowan—I mean everywhere. Worldwide. Anyone familiar with a certain kind of…'practice.' You don't like the word *performance*. But I think you know where I'm going: you're a…*some*thing."

"*Figure* is what I read. Someone said that."

"*Figure*. Good word."

"Better than *something*."

"I have a—I think—pretty shabby vocabulary."

"I'm a *teacher*. And you experienced that."

"I did."

"*Teacher.* And I don't diminish the word. Young fire and glass eaters come. Here. To me. Hoping I can bestow secrets. Which I can. Or can't. What I *can* do—and *try* to do, is to *indicate.* I'm sorry; I'm feeling extremely tired. Perhaps you could come back another time."

"Maybe tonight? Maybe later this evening?"

"I was thinking perhaps in a month or so."

"A month—"

"Or so."

Mr. Aquilla turned from me, moved again back toward his chair, sat, poured himself more of what we'd been drinking, drank, swallowed, rolled his head back, looked up at the sky. I wasn't sure exactly what I should do. So I followed him. He poured me a fresh cup. I drank it. I asked if I might ask just one last question before I left.

"Ask," he said.

"During those twenty-three, twenty-four years you were in Jiangxi Province," I began, "in prison. When you were tortured—"

"I wasn't tortured."

"I thought you said—"

"I was *tested*. There's a difference."

"Right, sorry; I see. Okay."

"What's the difference between a Blue Wing Olive and a Pale Morning Dun?"

He swirled the contents of his cup. Drank. Drained the cup.

I watched him, then looked at my hands. They looked hardened. Fired—like metal. They looked like somebody else's hands.

"I was tested," Anthony Aquilla repeated.

"In what way?" I asked.

Mr. Aquilla laughed.

Something angry, something urgent, uncoiled in me. "What I mean is—!" I began. "Was pain inflicted? Was blood drawn? Were you scarred? Starved?" I stood. I don't know why, but I stood. "Isolated?! Were there—I asked this before, but—were there notable *deprivations*?"

Mr. Aquilla turned. Looked at me. *Looked* is the wrong word; it was a *stare*. He put his hand to his mouth, began to shake his head. I could hear a deep, deep, muffled laugh behind his hand. "I'm sorry," he said. "I am. I've upset you. I didn't mean to. You asked: *Were there deprivations?* Robbie, young man—" He took the deepest breath I have ever seen a human being take. I imagined tribal reef divers staying underwater for inhuman lengths of time. He went on. "Please—" he began. "Deprivations? We *live* deprivations. Deprivations are the path we are born to. So, yes. *Deprivations.* Water. Food. Human contact. I was bled. I was sensorially bombarded. *Tested.* Repeatedly. For over twenty-two years."

"So...I guess the glass and fire became—"

"*Became?!* What?!" His words were like pistol shots. "Became *what?*"

"I don't—I don't know: a part, a part of—"

"Part of what?"

"Of *that.* Of combating your—"

Mr. Aquilla squared his body in front of mine. "My *deprivation?*"

"Yes."

He slowed his breathing. Shut his eyes. Opened them. "In what way?"

"I don't know. I guess—" I felt like a child. A being without language.

"Look, I'm *here,*" he said. "I slipped through. I endured; I lasted. Like a shadow, like a...sad song. Like a bad reflection. Endless cadence of light. Like a radical dream. Steam. I managed and lasted and slipped through. I eat fire. Last summer I swallowed at least two-thirds of California. I slipped through and lasted. I eat glass. I'm a recycler. I'm here. Did I not teach you anything just now?"

"You did."

"Did I not *guide* you?"

"You did."

"Don't you feel like you caught a very large fish?"

"I do. So: when you came back—"

"Oh, dear!"

"To here. No, please; hear me out. To this country. Where did you begin?"

"I'm tired."

"I'm sorry."

Anthony Aquilla slumped down in his chair. He looked like he might be sleeping. I waited. He lifted his head. "Have you gone yet?"

"No."

"He shut his eyes, opened them, drew his shoulders back. "I was at Wonderland at the start. And then Dreamland. I was in all the string shows, the ten-in-ones when they were only three-in-ones. I was a Sally and then a Bally. I had my breakfasts with Caliban, dinners with the Lizard Man and the Fat Lady. For a while I worked in blackface at Uncle Tom's. I saw what was possible at Hubert's. And I was at both the Chicago World's Fair and the Chicago fire. Who did *you* learn your guiding from?"

"I don't know. My father. Ricky at Ricky's Rafting River Trips." And then a list of others tumbled out. "Professor Steven Minot. Professor Lawrence Hall. Joseph Conrad. Franz Kafka. Willa Cather. John Cheever. I learned from them. Or tried to. What's the attraction? For you? In the crowd? What do you feel they *want*—the crowd—from you?"

Another deep breath. "Evidence that the world is not asleep," he said sternly. "Evidence that—just inside the flap of the tent—is living proof that the world can speak up and not repeat itself. A freak is one of a kind. A hero! We *stare* at the freak. We *observe* a crowd. How does a human being do this? Well, a human being *does* this because it is a deep need of human nature to think—*hope*—we are not simply that-which-is-presumed-of-us, that-which-is-expected. Come one! Come all! Come now! Come into the tent!"

He closed his eyes. Slept. I rose. Paused. Walked slowly to my car. Then stood in the approaching night, a moon shaved at its edges over my head. I smelled smoke. I heard the chiming of glass crystals. The bleating of goats and sheep. I left.

Epilogue

It's been three years. Almost. And I haven't gone back. To him, to Parowan and the rocky and raggedly planted hill that has Anthony Aquilla's home on it. To the goats grazing on the weed patches and Mr. Aquilla's tin cans.

I never published my interview. I never sent it out; it didn't seem right. Instead, I did a piece for the *New York Times Sunday Magazine* that I called "Secret Fly Fishermen." It was about famous people—men *and* women—who "go to church," as one of them put it, in both our little and great trout streams. Also, the *New Yorker* published a profile

I did called "Dale Chihuly's *Garden of Earthly Delights*." So I've been busy...putting one foot ahead of the other. Sometimes during the summer months I show up and either *guest-guide* or *ghost-guide* a day or two for Ricky on the Teton. I told him, "I'm keeping my toes in the water."

I have weird thoughts, though, now and again. Sometimes I imagine myself on fire. Sometimes I hear bleating in the next room. Sometimes my hands ache. And I have to soak them in hot water—often for a long time. Sometimes when I'm on the river my skin changes color and feels like leather. Sometimes when I breathe in I forget to breathe out. Sometimes I hear wind chimes and there's a taste in my mouth—partly of brandy, partly of blood. Sometimes I get the feeling I'm being tested...except nobody's there—nobody I can see—testing me. Sometimes I follow the weather news—all the fires and floods. And almost every day, it seems, I wonder—as I wondered that afternoon, on that hill in Parowan, starting out on my journey—where do the flames go?

The Resurrection of Ernie Fingers

Despite the timing—it was just barely post-pandemic—the Downtown Palace had nice opening reviews. Nothing soft, everything in place. Their three restaurants—if you trusted *Yelp*—merited a visit. The table odds were good. The slot selection and video poker were praised. They gave rooms away. They gave pint bottles of Jack Daniels away. They gave five-to-ten times points away to club players and offered twenty-to-one odds on certain bets at the dice table. Could a casino be more generous?

So where were the players? Bad karma? It was a conundrum.

"We need an attraction," Dickie Rice, the GM, said to Tony Padre, head of marketing. "We need crowds fighting to get in. We do that and who we are, what we offer will sell itself."

Tony Padre agreed. "Attraction! Absolutely! But what? Who?"

"You're possibly too young," Dickie Rice said. "But—any chance you remember Ernie Fingers?"

"Ernie—?"

"Fingers. Even as a kid—a *legend*. He would show up—out of *nowhere*—all the great lounges! Flamingo Room! Casbah at the Sahara. All! Sleight of hand. Probably the best sleight-of-hand artist I've ever seen. Jaw-dropping!" Dickie Rice mused. "And—Jesus—funny? His comic timing *had* comic timing! Hilarious. Opened—back in the day—for Lenny Bruce. Just a kid, maybe eighteen, nineteen. Trying to decide what he wanted. Whether to do stand-up or magic."

"So—?"

"Well...rumor is he's fallen on hard times. Still, people remember him. *Revere* him. Locals tell stories. You mention Ernie Fingers, and there's a whole—whaddya call it—*lore*. A whole mythology. His name alone is a magnet."

"So you thinking maybe we might—? Maybe could—"

"Right! See if we can find him. Feature him. We need an attraction. Desperately. A luminary. A draw. We could, I'm thinking, offer him the show room."

"Could. Except we don't *have* a show room."

"Well, we could possibly turn the *break room* into a show room. We'd have to clear it with corporate, but a *small* show room would work. Then, when he hits and even the scalpers have scalpers, we take the wall down between the break room and supply room. Seat maybe three, four, five hundred. Mystère—The Cirque show *made* the TI. Without Mystère, the TI would've tanked, would've gone down with their pirate ships. But you get yourself an attraction, you get yourself an amazement hour, and then! Then all the people who come... do *what*?"

"Play!"

"Exactly! *Become players!* Discover our restaurants, tell their friends. We'll run promotions! Give away rooms!" Dickie Rice unfurled his hands as if he'd witnessed a miracle. "We're huge! We're in the clover. What do you think?"

• • •

They met with Tony's PI, Scratch Carlotti. Dickie brought what he called his *Ernie Fingers file*: a couple of mentions in the Vegas *Review Journal*, a few more from the Greenspan Media Group. He'd found a couple of pictures; in both it looked like Ernie's face had been fashioned from Play-Doh. The only real lead came from a cocktail waitress who said she'd seen Ernie passed out in a far corner of Arizona Charlie's on Decatur.

Scratch hired on: $50/hour if he didn't find Ernie Fingers; found, his fee jumped to $300. The next day he called to report there were rumors. "All the stuff that's out there is dark," he said. "One rumor: He was badly burned... but survived. Another: He was entombed... but managed to escape. Still another had him being blinded and crippled by casino thugs because of debts."

"But no sense of *where*—?" Dickie began.

"I have a lead," Scratch said. "I'll call tomorrow."

Scratch's *lead* was to a place called Caliente-Caliente—a North Vegas video-poker bar, where he talked to a bartender named Slim whose pocked face looked like a golf ball. Slim recalled Ernie Fingers as all crusted and sere—a man who would slouch until he and the bar merged. "I actually varnished him one night!" Slim said. Slim conjectured that Ernie might still have a room at the Filthy-10, an infested motel complex near Nellis Air Force Base. Or—second guess—it was possible that Ernie Fingers lived in a supply-room locker at Ellis Island Casino on East Flamingo.

Scratch relayed his intel to Dickie Rice. "Would seem he still exists," Scratch said. "Not *well*, but—"

Dickie Rice was encouraged. Okay! The point was Ernie Fingers was out there! Findable! He felt new hope. He urged Scratch to stay on the chase.

Tony Padre made up and distributed SAVE THE DOWNTOWN PALACE buttons. Seeing all the employees with the buttons on their vests made you smile. There was a new lightness on the floor. A sense of possibility.

Scratch went back and bore down on Slim the bartender, who suggested talking to a woman named Lana, who dealt poker at the Stratosphere. Slim said she was psychic. Scratch found her. Did the name Ernie Fingers mean anything to her? *Yes.* Had she ever seen Ernie perform? *She had.* When? *Sixteen years ago, June 17, midnight show at the Backdoor Lounge in New York, New York*. Had she seen him since? *Yes.* How recently? *October.* This year? *Yes.* Where? *The Tuscany*. Doing what? *Card tricks at a back table in Marilyn's Café*. Anyone watching? *Only security*. Was he still good? *She wasn't close enough to tell*. But you're psychic. *He was brilliant*. Where can I find him? *Living in one of the Extra Space storage units on Rainbow*. What unit number? *Somewhere between 207 and 212*.

• • •

Rice and Padre found Ernie Fingers in storage unit 211. They'd followed someone with the gate code into the yard, and when they heard The Who's *Tommy* blasting from 211, they figured chances were it was Fingers.

They knocked. *See me!* Knocked again. *Feel me!* Then heard the music being turned down and movement. There was a sequence of bumping and fumbling. Finally—the sound of lock tumblers—clicks and slides and disengagements. The door vibrated. Folded on itself like brute origami. Clattered up.

Inside, a shadow, a shape swayed briefly, surged, then retreated—a shade backing into the black.

"Mr. Fingers," Dickie Rice tried, then—indicating to Padre that he should follow—stepped into the vault. Padre scanned with an LED pen flashlight until the beam found he-who-they'd-come-in-search-of huddled in a corner—more shape than person: dry and dark, charred and gnarled, like a bad night on a burn unit—head, body, and limbs more a mound of compost than a man. Scattered around were peels, rinds, grounds, bones, cores, blighted leaves. As well: spilling from black plastic bags were bottles—almost all bearing the same label, *Chopin Rye vodka*. And there was a stench.

"Sir—? Mr. Fingers—?" Dickie Rice probed.

"Mmm...?" Fingers droned, his voice like grass cuttings.

"Sir, my name is Rice. Dickie Rice. And this is my associate, Anthony Padre. We come as...past *admirers* of your work and hope that we might have a word. We have an offer."

They'd brought a package of chicken tenders as an offering. Ernie fed as the two outlined their cause, beginning with a mixed appetizer of nostalgia and praise: *I saw you at... I remember when you... One night you took a deerskin glove from a lady and turned it into a...*

Then Rice and Padre made their pitch. *Anything Ernie Fingers needed* would be provided: equipment, a suite at the Downtown Palace, stage staff, marketing, round-the-clock assistants, *name it!* And...how did he feel about publicity? Could they start press releases? If so, when? And assuming all went well when they expanded the show room, they would call it the Ernie Fingers Theater. Or—if that seemed self-centered—he could name it himself.

"What we were most hoping..." Here, Rice and Padre checked one another: *who should finish the sentence?* Padre, as marketing director, stepped up. "What we were most hoping is that—however you do it—you can make every person who's in attendance and who's watching you feel like a winner. Feel like winning is possible at the Downtown Palace. Feel like they can—as soon as your show's over—go out there on the floor and win. Win-win-win!"

Ernie Fingers said nothing. Dickie Rice filled the silence. "How's that sound? Like something you'd possibly be interested in? Something you'd be willing to take on?"

There was the sound that thought makes, the sound of chewing. "What did you say you called these things?" Ernie Fingers asked.

"Chicken tenders."

"Chicken tenders," Ernie Fingers repeated. And then again, one syllable at a time: "Chicken tenders."

• • •

They talked. They negotiated. They struck an agreement. There was a Discovery Inn just north of the storage complex. They'd begin there, clean Ernie up—hose him down, ply him with Prell and Listerine. Then they'd all drive downtown, introduce him, outline the space that would become his show room. They'd set him up with a laptop, establish an email so that they might send him PDFs.

PDFs?

Never mind. Next they'd get him a wardrobe—both casual and professional. Could he please write down any special needs? Best—in the event he presently lacked one—to get a bank account. They would advance two months' salary. And he'd be given a corporate credit/debit card. Was he familiar with—?

He was.

They understood that all of what they were asking and expecting must seem rushed, but the plan was to announce his opening in just over a month. And they were hoping—in fact corporate had made it a requirement—that Ernie Fingers would spend a week in rehab before assembling his show. Would that work? Would that be possible?

It would. Sure.

So Ernie Fingers signed, and they began. In the process, Dickie Rice asked Ernie Fingers: "All the bottles I saw, pretty much—at least those on the floor—were—"

"Chopin Rye," Ernie Fingers said. Then elaborated. Confessed. "I have a problem with Chopin. In particular Chopin Rye vodka. It's like an irony allergy," Ernie Fingers said and laughed.

Neither of the two casino executives got it.

• • •

Washed and groomed and clothed, Ernie Fingers checked into the Yellow Willow Hollow Rehab Center. Rice and Padre helped transport his cargo—duffle bags and new laptop—to his room. They set up a Gmail account for Ernie and held a review session on how to use the internet. Clearly Ernie wasn't completely new to the computer; he knew how to move—what keys and combinations led him to *where*. But his hand—wrist to fingertips— shook. In fact, his arms shook. His shoulders. "I'll be fine," he said, "fine. Just give me a day... two." A member of the Yellow Willow Hollow staff, Lolly, promised to help.

When the two Downtown Palace execs left, Ernie's only request was that—each day—they bring him a large bag of chicken tenders. "You can leave them at the reception desk," he said.

• • •

And so the rehab of Ernie Fingers began. His *resurrection*. As did hurried construction of what would be called the Ernie Fingers Show Room.

And after only two days at Yellow Willow Hollow, Ernie bloomed. He grew energized and computer-savvy—receiving PDF builder designs and specs as well as photos from every angle. He had ideas. And thoughts. And corrections.

Someone at Palace's corporate was a friend of Vegas's ex-mayor, Oscar Goodman. Goodman had seen and loved Ernie when he'd been just a lounge rat/magician/comic and was willing to do a short blurb in the Sunday *Review Journal*'s arts section. Another former mayor, Jan Jones, declared Ernie Fingers a "Las Vegas fringe underground legend." Finger's first week sold out. Then his second. Phone calls poured into a new Downtown Palace extension, the box office. *How'd you find him?...I remember seeing him at...He was the most amazing...!*

"I think we've found our attraction," Dickie Rice said—giving Tony Padre a man-hug.

"Let us pray," Padre said. And winked.

• • •

A week after Ernie had checked into Yellow Willow Hollow, he and Rice and Padre had a release meeting with the doctors.

"Amazing," a Dr. Patel said.

"Unbelievable," a Dr. Ludwig said.

"Decent reviews!" Ernie Fingers observed.

"He has a curious malady," the doctor in charge, a Dr. Donatello, stepped in. "Yes, he is alcoholic. Yes, one drink and the whole skein unravels. But—!" He held a forefinger dramatically in the air. "But—! It is only *one*, singularly *one*, brand and distillation—Chopin's Rye vodka—which undoes him! As a clinical study, we gave him Maker's Mark. Nothing. Glenlivet. Nothing again. Tanqueray. Nothing a third time! No excess. No intolerance. *Then* we gave him Chopin Potato. We gave him Chopin Wheat. The results were not quite as unequivocal, but there was no measurable distress. Chopin *Rye*, on the other hand—absolutely deadly! Off the chart! And especially if accompanied by Chopin's Nocturne in E-flat. Killer! I have no explanation. Without Chopin Rye vodka and his nocturne, Mr. Fingers is a man of high alcohol tolerance. He can drink almost…*almost*! anything and handle it. But he must not—*must not*, under any circumstances—be exposed to Chopin Rye vodka. Chopin Rye vodka is the Judas Iscariot of his spirit-world."

• • •

When Rice and Padre paid Ernie's' bill, they promised Yellow Willow Hollow to be his guardians and drove him straightaway to the suite they'd outfitted at the Palace. "Would you like a rental car?" Tony Padre asked. And then: "Do you drive?"

What they settled on was a driver named Carlos and a Downtown Palace stretch limo.

• • •

The two executives were struck by how different Ernie Fingers seemed now than when they'd discovered him in the storage unit. They referred to the Old Ernie and the New Ernie. The Old Ernie had been barely vegetative. The New Ernie seemed assured, even expansive. "Do you think maybe they've given him something?" Tony Padre asked. "The folks at Yellow Willow Hollow?"

"You mean like—?"

"I don't know," Tony said. "Like...I don't know. *Some*thing. Modern medicine."

"I guess exceptional is exceptional, genius...genius," Dickie Rice said.

• • •

Certainly there was no question: freed from rehab, the New Ernie was operating full throttle—both on his "The Return of—" show and his feedback on the design of the show room. He wanted casino equipment onstage. A blackjack table. A craps table. A roulette wheel. Specific slots. *Deuces Wild. Wheel of Fortune.*

Absolutely critical, he said, would be a camera that could film the show in real time and project it—magnified—onto a monitor readable to the audience. Any roll of the dice should be visible to the audience. Any card dealt in a blackjack game should be clear. Any machine spin should come up—projected in high resolution—for the audience to share. "I want the audience to feel," he said, "that magic is gaming; gaming, magic."

When Ernie said this, Dickie Rice shot an elbow into the ribs of Tony Padre.

The Palace found Ernie a tailor. The image he hoped for, Ernie said, was something between Houdini and Garth Brooks—something at once formal and informal—simultaneously denim and silk. During the fitting he held his hands elegantly in front of him like a pianist's, his digits leaping and separating from one another like the limbs of ballet dancers in *Swan Lake*.

But then, suddenly, both hands cramped—deformed and twisted. And with that, Ernie Fingers contorted himself, started making wounded animal sounds. "Jesus Christ, I *hate* this!" he said. "*Hate* it!

All of a sudden sometimes my hands treat me like an enemy! It's the Chopin. All those years of Chopin. The fucking Chopin has alienated me from my hands!"

Then, again and violently, in a kind of torque of his body, his hands quieted; his fingers danced. "Magic," he finally said. "Sometimes my middle finger *goes, just disappears* when I'm doing this. Once I lost my entire left hand. But time has taught me: *Don't worry.* All that vanishes will, one day, reappear."

His tailor said, "Please; just stand still."

• • •

The show room shape-shifted and then shape-shifted again like some golem, some form-finding creature in legend. It stopped simply being a space and became a transformational *zone*. In it, objects seemed lighter, heavier. Darker, lighter. Wider, sleeker, more tapered. Almost with a life of their own...then inert.

When Ernie asked why Rice and Padre had sought him out, they told him it was because he was a legend.

"My, my: a legend!" Fingers laughed. "A legend! Ah, me, mythology!"

• • •

At a week out—around the clock for the first three days—light technicians wrestled with clamps, lamps, and dimmers. Gels, cables, and adaptors. For the final stretch of four days, Ernie Fingers asked to be left alone in the show room. If he needed sleep, he'd sleep there. Should he hunger, he'd order in. Please: let him make his preparations. Please: leave him to his muse.

Every now and then Rice or Padre would set an ear to the show room door. Sometimes they'd hear music. Sometimes laughter. On occasion there was what sounded like animals—two by two—boarding Noah's Ark. Once when Dickie Rice cracked the door, Ernie was writhing on the floor, his hands clawing at the space above. *Be my friends! Be my friends!* Ernie was pleading with his fingers.

"What if he orders in from Lee's Discount Liquors and goes back on the Chopin Rye?" Padre asked.

"I don't think Lee's delivers," Rice said. "And you've gotta trust who you've gotta trust who you've gotta trust."

"What's that mean?" Padre asked.

"I have no idea," Dickie Rice said. "But I'm as terrified as you."

• • •

Then, finally, it was opening night! And then the first week...the second. Reviews appeared: in the *Review Journal*, the *Tribune*, the *Sun*. Shows were broadcast: KSNV, KLAS, KTNV. Everyone seemed in awe. Getting a ticket for Fingers Night of Casino Magic was nearly impossible. The only tickets were those Ernie produced at his fingertips and distributed among audience members.

"I've made friends with my hands," Ernie Fingers announced at the end of opening night.

• • •

And he had. He began his show simply—old and standard tricks made new. Like your uncle who produced quarters from your ears, your hair, and under your chin, Ernie Fingers wove a path through the audience, plucking and then gifting green ($25) and black ($100) chips. He reached behind the backs of women and suddenly had a Heidi Klum or a Cosabella bra in his hand. He would slip men's ties from their necks without untying them. He'd throw a tie into the air and it would come down a more expensive tie. A Countess Mara. "Winner-winner!" Fingers would announce.

Wandering though the audience, he stopped by a man wearing a ragged jacket. "You didn't dress for my show?" Ernie asked. The man apologized. In a single gesture, Ernie had the man's jacket in his hand. "Man as good looking as you—" Ernie began, and then he tossed the ragged jacket into the air. At the top of its arc there was a flash of light, and when the jacket descended it was an Armani. "I have the best tailor in Las Vegas," Ernie announced and handed the jacket back. "Try it on," Ernie commanded. The man did; "Perfect," he said. "I can reverse the trick," Ernie said. "Get your other jacket back." "No, I'm happy," the man laughed. "Winner-winner!" Ernie announced. And moved on.

And as he wove through the audience—making everyone feel like a winner-winner—he would employ his impressionist skills, slipping from voice to voice. He'd encounter one audience member as Jim

Carey, the next as Dolly Parton, the next as Johnny Depp. With these shifts, his entire face would become plastic and he would even *look* like the person he was impersonating. It was uncanny.

He had asked for casino tables. Which had been supplied. So he would invite a volunteer to—say—sit at the blackjack table, where the player was given two green chips. Some players, trying for a laugh, would say something like, *Is that all?* and Ernie Fingers would respond, "We'll see." As requested, all the play was televised; anyone in the audience could see it on a flat screen. The shuffling was elaborate and extremely thorough.

The cards were dealt. Fingers, as dealer, would show a 10. The player from the audience would have a stiff hand—14, 15, 16. "You'd better hit it," Fingers would advise. The player would get a 3. "Again," Fingers would suggest. The count would get to 18, 19. "Again," Fingers would advise, then "again." A player would have a 20, and Fingers would suggest, "Again." And the player. "Stick," Fingers would say. And he'd turn his hole card up and it would be a queen or jack or king. "Winner-winner," Fingers would say and pay. "Parlay," Fingers would advise, and soon the player would have several hundred in chips in front of her. Again and again—even with elaborate shuffling—the player would win. "When the show's over, take those out to the cage," Fingers would suggest. And the session would end.

At the craps table—same thing. A volunteer would choose dice. Roll them. Establish a number and make it. Then he would have six consecutive rolls that turned up either a 7 or an 11—after which, with the same dice, he would roll a 4 and then, on the following roll, repeat it. "Press!...Parlay!" Fingers would urge. Five minutes later the player, who had started with maybe $10, $15, or $20, would have several hundred. "The cage is to the left of the entrance doors," Fingers would offer. And then: "Winner-winner!"

"Everyone wins at the Palace," Fingers would shout, night after night, to the rafters.

As well, everyone won with Ernie's onstage slots. The Deuces Wild would produce four deuces on two or three consecutive spins. "You think this machine's rigged?" Ernie Fingers would ask. Then he'd pluck another audience member and give her $20. The new player would try and try and try and get terrible hands. Then he'd have the winning player hold his hand over the head of the new player. And four deuces would appear.

Winner-winner!

In between his casino magic, Ernie did impressions. He'd move upstage, cover himself with a shroud, appear to melt down into a puddle almost, then—whipping the shroud aside—arise as some famed Vegas performer: Elvis, Sammy Davis Jr., Sinatra, Liberace. But his impressions weren't only of men. He did Channing, Streisand, Dionne. His performance was an eerie and mesmeric mélange of transformed faces and body tics. On several occasions a resort physician had to be called in for an audience member whose disbelief rose to shock.

Dickie Rice asked Ernie if he might make his impressions just a bit less *real.*

"It's not within my control," Ernie apologized. "It's who I am. What I do. Tell your customers I'm sorry."

• • •

Post-show, Ernie would wander the floor, roam the casino, stop and watch players, put his hands on their shoulders. Whenever he did that the player's luck would improve. "Everyone wins at the Palace," Ernie would announce.

"How does he do that shit?" Tony Padre would ask. And Dickie Rice would just shake his head. "Can you believe these crowds?" Rice would say. "Did you ever imagine anything *like* this? Amazing!"

• • •

One of the regular giveaway tricks Ernie Fingers did involved booze. He would balance his magician's wand on the palm of his hand. Next he'd place a colorful silk over it. Then he'd point to an audience member: *The blond lady wearing the Hopi squash blossom and green sweater—what's your name, darlin'?* Or: *The gentleman in the fifth row wearing the black and yellow beach shirt—who made your hair disappear?*

Then—still balancing his silk-draped wand—he'd ask the inducted volunteer's liquor preference. A drink of choice would be named; Ernie Fingers would whip the silk away, and—in place of the wand—would be a full bottle of *whatever*: Tanqueray Ten, Johnny Walker Black, Gran Patrón Platinum Tequila.

One night a man who looked like Tom Hanks (and, as it turned out, *was* Tom Hanks) named his favorite cabernet: *Duckhorn*. "What year?" Ernie asked. "2006!" Tom Hanks shot back. *Whoosh!* The silk lifted like a bird. And there—replacing the wand—was a bottle of Duckhorn, which Ernie walked into the audience and presented. "I'm not wearing my glasses," he said. "Could you please tell me the year?" And Tom Hanks read: "2006!" "Enjoy!" Ernie said and the show moved on.

Some nights a smart-ass would name a *mixed* drink: *gin and tonic!* Or *Bloody Mary!* Or *fog cutter!* ("With or without the pineapple garnish?"/"With.") *Whoosh! Whoosh! Whoosh!* Gone was the silk, and there was the mixed drink. Audiences reeled! "Winner-winner!" Ernie would announce.

• • •

And so it went for over a month—standing room only. Ernie shone evening after evening. In the show room and afterwards strolling the casino floor. At any moment inside the Palace walls there was an almost electrical crackle of anticipation. Ernie would appear! He would *dis*appear! He would touch someone, and they'd win!

Where did Ernie go when he left? No one knew. He never answered a call. He rarely seemed to be in his suite.

Dickie Rice felt smug. He and Tony Padre gloated. Management started dropping by—sometimes with corporate—and both were dumbstruck. *You said you were going to bring an attraction—but you didn't say An Attraction.* Corporate flew the two to L.A. and treated them like heroes. "Somehow you've done the impossible," they were told. "Well—I guess that's what a magician does," Dickie Rice offered. Then added: "And a good casino."

• • •

Then, in the seventh week, an unsettling event occurred. It was during Ernie's wand-to-favorite-beverage trick. "Okay!" Ernie said, scanning the crowd, "Who needs a drink?"

"I do!" a gruff voice—a voice raw and cruel—boomed from the back. Heads spun. The source was a grimy man in a tattered overcoat.

Some alarm went off in Ernie; he struggled to maintain his usual ease. "Anyone else?" he said. "Thirsty? A drink?"

"Chopin Rye vodka!" the grisly man barked.

"Glenlivet! Highland Single Malt!"

Swoosh! and the wand became a bottle of Glenlivet Highland Single Malt—which Ernie presented.

"I asked for Chopin Rye vodka!" the grimy man roared.

"Yes—but so rudely. And manners count," Ernie quipped. The audience laughed. And the hunched, grungy man skulked from the theater.

But Ernie Fingers knew: he'd be back.

And he was. The next night. And the following night. "Chopin Rye vodka!" *The Spook*. On the third night, from a small boom box, came Chopin's Nocturne in E-flat.

Ernie stopped. Stood in his spotlight. Calculated. Considered. Except for the Chopin, the room was without sound. Then, finally, Ernie Fingers called: "Security!"

Security moved. Ernie pointed. The man and his boom box were removed—after which Ernie stood, silent and thoughtful, on the stage. "So...what? Where were we?" Ernie asked. And he moved on to the grand finale of his show.

• • •

Word reached Rice and Padre about the Chopin man, so they scheduled room-service breakfast with Ernie in his suite: prime-rib hash, Irish oatmeal, lox, eggs Benedict, popovers and jam. "If there's something that you don't see but that you want—say so. It's yours!" Dickie Rice said.

They asked Ernie if he knew who the man was and why he'd materialized. "Any idea?"

Ernie had none. Not true, though: he had an inkling. "Sometimes," he said, "I send very dark spirits to *myself* to see whether I can handle them. It's possible that I'm the person who *is* the person... who won't go away."

"In which case—" Dickie Rice began.

"In which case," Ernie said, "I'm going to have to make him *disappear.*"

"And if you can't?" Tony Padre asked.

"And if I can't…and if I can't, it will mean I'll have to disappear myself. I mean, I've done it before. I can do it again."

"But how would you do that?" Tony Padre asked.

"A magician never reveals his tricks," Ernie Fingers said. And smiled.

Ernie insisted that he was feeling strong and believed that he needed to test himself. The grisly man was to be allowed back into the show room when he came next. "I've been doing tai chi. And some strong somatosensory exercises," Ernie said. "I think I'm ready. For him. My *Spook.*" Ernie laughed—a dark laugh, an empty laugh—but a laugh nevertheless.

Rice and Padre pledged their presence. Vigilance. "Count on us. We'll be back there. In the standing-room section. And we'll triple the security detail," Dickie Rice assured.

• • •

That night again the man came—less a body, more a shadow—one member of security to his left another to his right. The show began, moved along; Ernie Fingers was brilliant, his hands like hummingbirds. Then came the late moment when he asked for spirit preferences.

"Chopin Rye vodka," came the raw and squalid call from the nearly fungal shadows at the back.

"I'm hearing *Chopin Rye vodka,*" Ernie replied slowly, almost chewing on each syllable.

"You got it: *Chopin Rye vodka*!"

The ensuing silence was almost surgical. Then Ernie said something. Then the Spook spoke. To which Ernie replied. To which the Spook answered. There was no sense to be made of the exchange. All the sounds, words, whatever they were—these *issuings* of first one and then another throat—guttural, indecipherable, like the night sounds snaking out of an alligator pit or great-ape house, were *gibberish.*

Back and forth the demonic and Precambrian sounds went—Ernie balancing his silk and wand on the palm of his hand: first the grisly man, then Ernie—bestial, brutal, fiendish.

Then Ernie snapped the silk, and there in his palm stood a bottle of Chopin Rye vodka—suddenly backgrounded by the great musician's Nocturne in E-flat.

"Aha!" Ernie's Spook barked out.

"Aha!" Ernie shot back.

"How does it feel to have it once again in your hand, so close… so close to your throat?" the Spook asked over the nocturne's legato.

"It feels inevitable!" Ernie replied. His eyes looked like lead weights, like Murano glass.

"Toss it to me. I'll catch it!" the Spook taunted.

Ernie tried to toss the bottle, but it wouldn't leave his hand.

"C'mon, pitcher-pitcher, Mr. Magic: toss it!" the Spook sneered. And he squatted. Waited. Stood.

Ernie, as if sleepwalking, moved toward the man.

Palace security started closing in.

"Hand it to me!" the Spook jeered.

There they were—twenty, fifteen, ten feet apart—Ernie extending the Chopin, offering it out…and out. But the bottle wouldn't leave his fingers. And now the twisted and deformed shape was laughing. A good quarter of the audience were screaming. It was high horror. It was *Alien* meets *Silence of the Lambs.*

What happened next—though the Palace's surveillance cameras mapped every inch of the space—remains unclear. Renditions vary. So much is *in* or *not in* the eye of the beholder. Still, there is a vague and scattered agreement about certain elements. *Crackling light*—as though the room's entire electrical system were shorting. *Visceral bodily shrieks* or bellowings. *Laser-like beams.* Riotous *sounds of breakage*—particularly glass. *Pulsing images* of blood and naked flesh. The *reek* of spilled alcohol. The entire duration of the episode (known because a member of security stop-watched it) clocked in at a minute and seven seconds only.

Suddenly normalcy was restored—lights, air-conditioning, sound system, the Kenny G soundtrack that had been playing before all in the show room had collapsed. The audience began to resettle. Security stood in the aisles—scanning. Then, abruptly, everyone saw and realized: Ernie Fingers lay in a heap on the apron of his stage.

A collective breath caught in a universal throat. If there is a music that might be called a *music of carnage*, it did a kind of scorched-earth of Kenny G and screamed from the far corners of the room. Ragged shards of glass glistened like some kind of cruel throw rug on the stage. But then...slowly at first, then with greater and greater possession and agility and dignity, Fingers rose from where he'd curled, crumpled.

He looked out. Looked around. Saw that his Spook was gone. Smiled.

And then he hunched and removed his shoes—slowly, first one and then the other. He took off his socks. Finally—with a broad smile—he wove a path over the strewn glass shards. The audience heard the broken brittle glass breaking into smaller pieces. Snapping. The glass was like a kind of *stilled water* everywhere. It seemed a transport beyond magic. It seemed a miracle.

Then—Ernie Fingers stopped. He held a hand out. A dove appeared at his fingertips and stayed there. Still. Motionless. Like a tamed nightmare or memory. "End of show," Ernie Fingers said. The lights dimmed. The audience rose and applauded. And when the lights relit, Ernie was gone.

• • •

And so the attraction that Dickie Rice and Tony Padre had sought and needed, Ernie Fingers, disappeared. Yet what he'd inspirited at Las Vegas's Downtown Palace lingered on. Sometimes only as flickering as hope. Other times as strident as gratitude.

And those who knew, those who'd been there, seen Ernie Finger's performances, swore that there were times they saw him still—saw him step up behind a player at a dice or card table, or a gambler at a Wheel of Fortune, and touch that player on the shoulder, wish him, wish her, good luck. And the player would win.

And after all, isn't winning—in whatever disguise and at whatever odd hour, on any off night—what any of us hold our breath for?

The Photojournalism Project

Melissa Probert was a binge drinker who had been Leah's friend first. Then Hunt's. Now she alternated between them—Leah more when she was sober, Hunt when she was drunk. She was a freelance journalist who was in and out of town, and when she'd call and check in was anybody's guess.

So when the phone rang and Hunt answered, who could have predicted it would be Melissa—drunk and raging with self-loathing? Her questions poured, like indiscriminant gin, over her own head: *Had she no reverence for her gifts? Did she think power was easily come by? In two years, if she kept careening, would she even be able to compose a shot? And finally: Would Hunt come by to talk?*

Hunt said sure; he had to clean his brushes, but give him an hour and he'd be over. He was doing a tempera series of roadside shrines. The note he left for Leah said, "At Melissa Probert's" and gave her number.

• • •

In the time between her call and Hunt's arrival, Melissa had finished her Metaxa and was well into some Calvados. "No cheap shit for me," she said. Her hair crisscrossed her face; the gray, in just two weeks, seemed to have run rampant. It was hard to know whether she was answering the door or using it to stay vertical. "*Entrez!*" she said. "I'm a fucking mess!"

Hunt thought of saying: *Well, I've seen you this way before*, but it seemed ungracious.

"Well, I guess you've seen me this way more than once," Melissa said. "Want a drink?" And she laughed. She had at least six cameras set and ready on tripods. "Photo madness!" she announced, sweeping her arm; "photo mania! Photo post-postmodernism!"

Melissa Probert was, in fact, highly respected as a photojournalist. Probably she was among the ten most sought after in her field. More than once Hunt had been at her home when the phone rang and it had been: *Get your bright ass and cameras over to Iraq or Nicaragua*; most recently she'd been summoned to Beijing. Some weekly once owned by Rupert Murdoch or Time-Warner always needed her images posthaste. Her way of seeing almost any shocking event around the world placed her in demand, caused her to be called away. Above that, her photos hung in MOMA—and in Boston, Dallas, at the Hirshhorn, the Art Institute of Chicago. They flooded the West Coast. Hunt had seen her work hung next to David Hockney's.

But Melissa Probert also had what people *with it* often call *a problem*. She drank. Over last two years she'd been drinking more. And more. And then often, when that was done, more again. She understood the danger. She understood the impairment. She was losing work; she was losing calls; worst, she was fast losing her self-respect. "Look at me! I am fucking trashing the single power that I have!" she had said on more than one occasion.

And she was—especially while occupying the interior of her problem—frankly calamitous with men. Shaggy and wasted *would-bes*—would-be writers, would-be composers (would-be *actors* were the worst!)—thundered in and out of her house. "If I were smart, I'd just buy a German shepherd and embrace bestiality," she'd told Hunt.

Melissa felt safe with Hunt, and Hunt with her. They understood each other, although their shortcomings spoke different languages. So that was why Melissa Probert had called Hunt: to propose that he help her, sustain her in a critical photojournalism project that, as she saw it, she would then be able to roll over directly into a book (she had two photo books already—one with Random, the other with New York Graphic—and a contract for a third).

And the project—*should he choose to accept it*—Hunt would help her with was: she would photograph her next drunken episode and be relentless—the bile, the need, the ugliness, the violence, the despair: herself, in shot after shot, ruining herself, having no respect for her god-givens. "So if you'll just *be* here," she said, "as my friend...as my friend to insist and see that I don't back off. That I *do* it. And that I go the distance. And when I can't point a camera, when I can't set up a shot...*you* point it, *you* set it up. *You* take the roll from every angle. The puffy face. The spittle. The nerveless lips."

She said the project, as she saw it, was in the tradition of all the great literary confessions—Augustine, Rousseau. "If I humiliate myself *enough*, deeply *enough*—publicly, professionally—see my wretched abuse there on people's coffee tables...then I know I'll stop. It will bring me *to* that. Will you do it?"

Hunt made an O with his lips. He wasn't sure what the grimace meant; nothing came out of it. He said he'd try. He said he'd do his best.

Melissa stumbled against him, hugged him, nearly knocked him down. "This isn't *it*," she said. "This isn't the one. This is just a warm-up. This is just the aerobics of alcoholism, just a day bender." She laughed and struck a prizefighter's stance, punched him not so lightly on the jaw. Her large jagged-silver and amethyst ring caught him in a fold of skin and sliced him.

• • •

Hunt told Leah that night over blush wine and chicken breasts what he'd been conscripted into. "So it's basically a photojournalism project," he said. "Giving Melissa a...really, I guess, a minor hand in her next book."

"I've seen you give a minor hand before," Leah said. "I'm less than encouraged." Leah recalled the time when, invited to Melissa's for chimichangas, she and Hunt had walked in on Melissa and a man who, ever since, Leah had referred to as "Hairy Shoulders"—the two locked in (again Leah's memorialized phrase) *sportive glee*. "Hunt?" Leah abruptly asked, "is that dried blood under your left eye?"

"It's an old fencing wound," Hunt offered. "Unconnected with sportive glee."

"Hunt, you could have 'sportive glee' and not know it," Leah jibed. Then apologized. Then gave Hunt the permission he was, indirectly, requesting. "Fine, sure, what the hell," Leah said. *Friends, after all, were friends; there were too few, finally, in the world. The notion needed encouragement. Hunt was (wasn't he?) his own person; if she said no, he'd only slip over at the zero hour anyway to help Melissa, so why not? Of course, sure, by all means help her chronicle her self-destruction.*

• • •

A day went by. Two. It felt a bit as if the electricity bill hadn't been paid and Leah and Hunt were waiting for the power to be turned off. And then one morning at breakfast their son Sean torqued the eye-of-the-storm feeling even more, offering: "Maybe I'll just forget college. Get a job. Live at home. What do you think?" He had a copy of Günter Grass's *The Tin Drum* just to the right of his latte.

The table was silent. Then: "There'd be rent," Hunt said.

"And baby-sitting fees," Leah added.

• • •

An hour later, what Hunt took to be Melissa Probert's call-to-duty came—because when he said *hello*, the line held a quizzical silence. "Hello?" Hunt tried a second time and then a third.

"Hunt?" asked a voice, tipsy but clearly not Melissa's. "Hunt? Hey!" it said. "Hey—hi! It's me!"

It was C. J. Robbs, and she was in Montana. "My fucking *ex*!" she said. "Darrell. He has my kids here on a vacation. I thought I'd circle the wagons. And I—it was amazing; I don't know how I did it, but I found their motel. I thought I'd wait until Darrell, you know, was at the Wagon Wheel with anorexic Annette, then sneak in and see them. I was in my car. All my shit. Oh: I'm on my way, by the way, to Tucson: how's that? Hunt?"

"Right. I'm here," Hunt said.

"Good. Good; that's where you sound—*here*... *there*. I was in my car. And I saw Bronson and Rachelle coming out of unit 12, heading to the diner. Which they went into. It was—I mean, I have to tell you—it was so exciting! To see them. So I put on makeup. Well... And I followed. Went in, came up behind them—they were drinking hot chocolate, eating sticky rolls—and I surprised them. And we hugged—it was amazing! Christ, I cried, screamed, talked loud. Pissed the waitress off, but fuck her—right?"

"Right."

"Good to hear your voice, Hunt."

"And yours. I tried to call."

"Disconnected—right?"

"Right."

"Well, that's me. Hey! Guess where I'm coming? Going—whatever."

"Where?"

"Tucson!"

"Really?"

"Did I say that? Just now? Before?"

"You did."

"Well, I figured I had a friend there."

"You do."

"So will you teach me? Lessons? In oils? I've been having dreams, and—well, partly this is embarrassing, but I'll skip the embarrassing stuff. Anyway, you've been instructing me. In various things."

"And oils is one."

"Right."

"So, what happened with your kids? When you surprised them?"

"Oh—fucking Darrell walked in. Blew a gut. Grabbed both kids by the backs of their shirts. Held them up like laundry. Told me—leave or he'd call the cops. Said I owed thirty-six hundred in child support. Said when he saw the thirty-six hundred, I could see the kids. I could've written a check, you know. From what I've sold. But the whole idea—kids watching while I hauled my checkbook out and, like some pathetic bitch, wrote their father a check—which anorexic Annette would just use for more fucking furniture... I couldn't do it."

"I understand," Hunt said.

"Of course you do," C. J. Robbs said. "Of course. That's why I'm calling you. And that's why I'm hauling ass to Tucson. Because you understand. Hey—what're you up to? What are you painting now?"

"Paintings."

"Right."

"No, I mean I'm painting paintings... of burning paintings. And some shrines."

"Cool!"

"Actually, right now, I'm waiting for a call from a photojournalist friend who has a drinking problem."

"Great! I have a drinking problem—drink all night; don't get drunk. Introduce us!"

"I don't think—"

"Listen, should I just *kill* Darrell and Annette? I know this guy—worked in the CIA. He said he could get exploding condoms. Wouldn't that be the cat's whatever? 'Cause then I'd just *take* the kids."

"I'd—"

"What?"

"Think on it. Give the plan—what you just said—breathing space," Hunt said, "before you—"

"I'm just kidding. I'm just kidding, Hunt," C. J. Robbs said.

"I knew that—I think," Hunt said.

"So, I guess: wait up for me, okay? I'll be there. Count the hours! You have a student."

"Fine," Hunt said. "I'll look forward to it. Meantime—travel carefully; take care."

"It was great seeing Rachelle and Bronson," C. J. Robbs said. "Even for ten fucking—I'm sorry—minutes. It was worth going to Montana. Annette treats Rachelle like shit. I *know*. She said, she told me: fucking Cinderella/stepmother shit. It hurts me. I can't tell you how it hurts me; it makes me nuts."

"Well—you'll get famous. Have more money than you can use. Get them back. I'll help you with that. All the money-making oil-painting techniques: I'm good at that." Hunt laughed.

"You know: I talk to you—you know...want to hear what I think?"

"Sure. Why not? Tell me."

"I think: *I have a friend*," C. J. Robbs said. She was crying.

"Well...that's right. Good. You do," Hunt said.

• • •

The next morning, Thursday, before breakfast, the phone rang. "It's one of your women," Leah said. "*Friends*," she semi-corrected. She handed the phone to Hunt.

"Hunt?" Melissa said, too near the mouthpiece.

Something distributed itself unevenly along Hunt's vertebrae. "Is this it?" Hunt asked.

"No," Melissa giggled. "No...just checking," she said. And she laughed. Oddly, strangely. "This is just...the word is *checking*. This is just...here we go: *civil defense*." She was a little drunk, clearly. "This is just to see if my friend is there and is still my friend."

"I'm here," Hunt said.

"I know," Melissa said. "I know. You are. You're sweet. Hey—but listen," she slurred on, "hey, listen: you're not *wait*ing on me, are you? You're not suspending any of your *own* work?"

"Well, no. I'm—no, no, I'm trying not to," Hunt said. "I'm trying to finish at least a canvas a week."

"Shrines." Melissa said, remembering Hunt's new series. Checking.

"Shrines," Hunt said. "Yes, right, shrines."

"Like where some drunk—right? am I getting this right?—has swerved into a power pole?" she asked. "Or crashed into some children getting out of a school bus...like I might do."

"Along those lines," Hunt said.

"And then they—*someone*—constructs this little, like, birdhouse thing, right? A *shrine*."

"Shrine. Yes."

"Right...with candles," Melissa Probert said. Melissa had this uncomfortable way of teasing. "Well, good then," she said finally. "Good. Good luck. Get back to them. *In* them. Whatever. Pursue your calling. Get back into your shrines." And she hung up.

"So was that *it* or *not it*?" Leah's words tiptoed over Hunt's shoulder as he stood, considering, by the phone.

"Uh, *not it*," he said, "*not*." Something in his brain eclipsed a fair portion of his voice.

"So do you have your shutter finger ready?" Leah asked.

"Leah, don't. Okay?" Hunt said.

"What's your aperture?" she asked.

"Please...look: Melissa's a very gifted photographer."

"And I'm a very gifted wife and fund-raiser," Leah said.

"Yes. And...?"

"So?"

"What's your point?"

"Precisely," Leah said and flexed her eyebrows. She poked the end of Hunt's nose with her finger and moved, using what looked like a dance step, into the kitchen. "Wine?" she said.

"Sure." Hunt heard the cabinet opening, bottles being redistributed, a cork slipping the lip of an opened bottle.

"So what kind of *duration*—when this happens—do you think we're talking about?" Leah called from the other room.

"I don't know," Hunt called back. "I guess...well, obviously, however long it takes."

"Oh! Right: the old 'however-long,'" Leah said. "A month? Six years?"

"I think more...*hours*, probably," Hunt said.

"Like how many?" Leah said. "Two? Three thousand?"

"Okay," Hunt said. "Okay, I get your point."

"Good—what is it?" Leah said.

• • •

The real, the *true* call came that same night—3 in the morning. "I lied," Melissa Probert said, her voice thin and barely able to wrap itself around the two syllables. "I can't make a *t* sound," she said. "I can't say: 'Tonight's the night.' I tried; I rehearsed. It kept coming out: 'nice-the-ni' or like 'nighty-nite' or 'mack the knife' or something."

"I'll be right over," Hunt said.

He leaned over the bed and told Leah, then started to dress.

"Will you write?" Leah asked. "Will you send a postcard? Is the insurance paid? the phone? the electricity? my Neiman card? Just in case?"

• • •

Melissa was, in fact, wasted, the house in ruins—bottles, laundry, garbage. This time, there were at least a dozen cameras: Nikons, Cannons, Leicas, a Voigtländer, an old shutter camera. "I got myself vomiting *dust*," Melissa said. "It was a great shot! Come in. Watch where you step."

She told him she had her whole house rigged: lines to cameras and rubber bulbs in the lines so that when you stepped on a bulb you triggered the flash and shutter. "It's like a goddamn *minefield*. she said. "Take a wrong step...you're—as they say—*history*!"

Hunt entered. The interior of Melissa Probert's house smelled like varieties of incontinence. There was broken glass. Both the television and a Bose CD player were blasting. Whatever the television program was, its horizontal hold was whacked, making card shuffles. Somewhere—some room, some closet—Hunt was sure he heard a dog barking. "Is there some animal in here?" he asked.

"Just me," Melissa Probert gurgled, then started choking.

Hunt rushed to hold her from behind, one hand across her abdomen, the other stroking her back. "Easy... easy," he kept saying until she slowed, slowed her breathing and quieted. "Easy..."

"Hey—it just *looks* easy," Melissa said and snorted when she got her voice back. "Want a drink?"

"No, thank you," Hunt said.

"Hunt—c'mon; don't be an asshole," Melissa said. "Don't be an asshole. Really. I didn't ask you over here to be that. Be a sport."

Hunt inventoried his role, his responsibilities. He shook his head.

Melissa wove a stumble to the counter, where she snatched up an uncapped Grand Marnier and took a slug from it. A flash went off. "Was that timing or was that timing?" Melissa said. She took another belt. A second flash popped. She raised the bottle above her head for a third illumination. "This is going to be a fabulous book!" she barked. "Fabulous!" She tried to laugh but started choking again. "Fuck!" was all she could say, the single syllable, single word: "Fuck!... Fuck!... Fuck!"

When Hunt tried to wrest the Grand Marnier from her, she elbowed him and twisted away, then held the bottle, once again, aloft.

"Grand Marnier!" she announced. "Grand Marnier! I'm cooking my own goose!" She laughed and choked, then managed, "This is for the reduction!" She tripped and fell over a fold in the Navajo rug. When Hunt rushed to help, she blared, "No! No! Use the Nikon! Use the Nikon on the table. The F2A. Bring it over. Hurry! Lie down on the floor! Start snapping! Good... good! Move around! Move around me! Keep shooting. Good. Good. God, I'm a fucking mess, aren't I?"

"You are," Hunt said.

Melissa rolled over onto her back. Grand Marnier spilled onto the rug and leaked over her blouse. She went to pour the little left into her mouth and got her eyes. "Shit—shoot it!" she yelled. "Shoot it, Hunt! Shoot it, quick!"

Hunt took half a roll. Melissa Probert blacked out. And with her loss of consciousness, a half dozen filament loops of tungsten flared then turned to ash in Hunt's uncertain brain.

• • •

First Hunt stood above her and steadied himself. Then he knelt, inclined, checked her breathing. It seemed regular, if not normal. And her throat appeared to be clear. Hunt stretched, slipped his arms under her, and lifted. Melissa vomited but didn't wake. The vomit balled in Hunt's alpaca sweater. Hunt stepped on one camera bulb, then another. Sequential flashes flared, capturing the moments. He carried Melissa to her couch. It was a nest of broken tortilla chips. He held her over one shoulder and brushed the chips to the floor, then set her down, her weight leaving him but not, the freight of it taut still down his arms, the sense of her woman's body not entirely neutral in his hands.

At first he observed only. Then he dropped silently to his knees, brushed the hair from her eyes. He positioned a small satin pillow and then a second under her midsection, her hips, his intent to make her comfortable and to open her breathing. Her facial features looked misplaced; her body seemed potentially weightless and insubstantial. What if she died?

• • •

While she lay passed out, Hunt did his best to clean up. He used Lysol and paper towels. Trying to sweep the floor, he set off at least a dozen more bulbs. Melissa rolled off the couch. Hunt stroked her face with a warm and lightly soaped cloth. He wrapped her in a blanket and gave her the wider berth of the hardwood floor. He took pictures or triggered her preset cameras at each point. He knew she'd be angry if he didn't. He washed dishes, made coffee. The sun came up, spilling a faint green haze into an otherwise clear day. Hunt wandered outside.

It was still. Too still. And breathless. It was a first hour void of any conviction about itself, lost from any resolve to become a day. It was a first hour knowing nothing better than to grow vaguely, chronically light.

Nothing stirred. Nothing skimmed the receptors of Hunt's skin even remotely. It was a dawn that seemed, in fact, to drain him, as he stood in it, of determination. Should he stay? Leave? Sleep? Work? Did it matter? Why had he come anyway?

People who allowed themselves to become shapeless, Hunt thought, *Jesus*!—though, to confess, he had no idea what he meant. Still something crouched over the whole situation made him feel fat and nearly useless. And he wanted to move. He wanted to put distance between himself and such feeling.

Instead he turned and went back in. Surveyed. There were still bottles everywhere, mostly cognacs, brandies, aperitifs. Hunt left each one where Melissa had dropped or set or tipped it. A few were empty but most still had liquor. Hunt washed the kitchen and bathroom floors, scrubbed remaining clots of sickness away with soaped wire pads. He turned the television off. He clicked the radio on for the morning news. A bakery truck had overturned: a major artery was slick with white bread and sweet rolls; the baker, who was driving his own truck and who had previous convictions for possession of cocaine, was in critical condition; travelers were being advised.

Again Hunt checked Melissa's breathing. It seemed more regular. He let her sleep. He went to her bookshelves, pulled down both her photography books, sat and leafed through them. *Jesus, she was good! She was good; she was so good!* One book was on Single Room Occupancy hotels. Different cities. Sad, brave, exhausted people boxed and diminished in minimal light: eyes hard as rivets, dilated, irises looking like question marks. Black and white. Both books: black and white. She refused color. That was interesting. They'd had this argument: *You guys, you painter guys use color. See, I'm a lab technician. I'm just... hanging around, looking for shadows in the tissue. You know what I'm saying. I'm just looking for the little stuff,... hairline bone cracks, trivia, that kind of stuff. I don't need color for that.*

• • •

Hunt called Leah at her work. Before he spoke he stashed a large breath. "She's out," he told Leah.

"Out of the house or out of her head?" Leah asked.

"Sleeping," Hunt corrected.

"I went down to your studio this morning," Leah said. "I looked at your new paintings." She paused.

Hunt waited in her pause. Anything was possible.

"The shrines," she said finally, then stopped.

"Right," Hunt said.

Leah said nothing.

"Yeah?" Hunt said. "And?"

"They're eerie," Leah said.

Hunt couldn't think what to say next, what his turn ought to be.

Leah took up the slack and moved ahead. "The candles," she said. "The black tree branches. The weeds. The inscriptions in...I presume, *Spanish*—are they religious?"

"The paintings?"

"Well, I think I was asking more about the words. They seemed to be."

"Probably," Hunt said.

"Well, and—since you directed my attention—are the *paintings* religious?"

"I...It's hard for me to know." Hunt said. "Ever."

"I realize that," Leah said, and Hunt was uncertain whether she said it sarcastically. "So then, now what?" Leah said. "You wait; she wakes up; you come home?"

"I'm not sure," Hunt said.

"Hmm," Leah said. "I see: *not sure*—like the paintings. So I guess what's going on over there is a religious experience...helping this drunk."

Hunt didn't want to say anything if he didn't have to.

"Hunt?" Leah prompted.

"I'm not sure how she'll feel. What she'll expect. Once she's woken again. Whether she'll feel the thing's over or not," Hunt said.

"The thing," Leah repeated.

"Her intention. Leah, you know what I mean. The objective."

"The humiliation."

"In part, I suppose, yes."

"Well, I guess I'll see you when I see you then," Leah said.

"Yes, I guess. I suppose that's the general scenario," Hunt said. And they hung up. Hunt kept his hand on the phone, Leah's fear, her edge, sharp against his palm.

He stayed that way for perhaps a whole minute. Then he unclenched, uncurled, and strolled to a row of Melissa's bottles, staggered in a vague line on a side table. He picked one up, tipped it, waggled it. There was a hefty shot, shot and a half, still there, and Hunt threw the whole of it back, feeling it sweet at first, then warm, then burning, finally choking inside his throat. He sucked the room's cooler air and thought if there were another shot, he would just as soon suck that in as well... and then another shot after that. There were times when a person, *any* person, any person at all, might just as easily stuff the neck of a bottle down his throat.

Hunt felt seized. He went into Melissa Probert's bathroom and threw up. When he wiped his face with her washcloth, he was careful not to see his own face in her mirror.

* * *

He leafed through Melissa's second volume. It was entitled *Grandmothers* and was, simply, that. All races, ages, socioeconomic status. How had she lit them? From the front? Behind? The side? Hunt couldn't tell. Still, there was something about the eyes.

The radio reported that the baker whose truck had crashed had a rare blood type. A search was on to find a match for a transfusion. He was still on the critical list, but slipping.

* * *

Melissa came around. She started rolling at first, side to side, on the floor. Hunt took pictures. She opened her eyes, wrenched herself to a sitting position, rocked back and forth. "You okay?" Hunt asked.

"Use the Leica," Melissa said. "It'll be the best one in this light."

Hunt did as instructed. Within ten minutes Melissa had pulled herself to her feet and was opening new bottles. "You're not through?" Hunt asked. Melissa shook her head. She had a bottle of Rémy Martin and was slugging it like a teenager guzzling milk. Hunt could nearly feel the alcohol surge firing in *him*. "Hey, that's a lot... *fast*," he said over the sound of the shutter, squeezing off a half dozen shots.

"Well, listen...listen, boyo," she said, "let me tell you: that's how it's done. *A lot fast*: it's the *only* way." She spread the fingers of her free hand over her head. "Don't miss this one," she said: "'Grotesquerie'....'Self-Mockery.'"

Melissa drank, off and on, for the next three days. She retched. She soiled herself. She and Hunt heard a bulletin reported the death of the baker. "Don't take it so personally," Melissa said to Hunt. She helped him change film. She broke bottles; she broke glasses; she hurled a half-drained Chambord decanter through her TV, a hanging fuchsia through a window. But always she made sure that, between them, she and Hunt captured every moment, every vile assault and humiliating scene. Each time she passed out, Hunt would clean up her mess—the spill, the vomit, the wreckage. Then she would wake—and spill and vomit and wreck again, ensuring at every step that it was all being recorded. They went through nearly two hundred rolls of film.

• • •

Hunt called home. Leah got more and more terse. "Where are you sleeping?" she asked.

"Well, just in a chair," Hunt said.

"And where does she sleep?"

"On the floor."

"Mmm," Leah said.

"What do you mean—*mmm*?" Hunt asked.

"I mean, and never the twain—right?" Leah said.

"I'm not sure what—" Hunt began, then drifted.

"I'm just observing," Leah said. "I'm just noting that there must be a lot of friendship there. I mean, three days' worth...with a drunk woman."

"Well, there's...yes; there's a fair amount, I think," Hunt said. And then he told Leah, his voice clogged suddenly, that he admired—if she were going to press it—yes: he admired, in fact, what Melissa Probert was attempting to do.

"Oh. You mean kill herself?" Leah said.

"No: I mean: *see* herself, face herself," Hunt said. He didn't back down.

"As opposed to whom?" Leah said, squeezing her lips down, more than casually, on the *m*.

"I don't think that I'm opposing it or her to anyone," Hunt said. "I just think there's a certain courage she has, that's all."

"Oh, I do too," Leah said. "I do too. And I think the world is a lesser place because there's not more confrontational self-abuse."

"You're angry," Hunt said.

"I think I'm pretty good," Leah said. "I think I'm, actually, quite a marvel...letting my husband spend three days with an alcoholic woman who fucks men indiscriminately."

"I'm not sure that's accurate," Hunt said.

"Oh, well, *accuracy*, of course, is the point-isn't it?" Leah said. "And by the way: who's C. J. Robbs? She called again." Leah hung up. Ten minutes later she called back, crying, and apologized. "I just want you to know that I think *I'm* doing a courageous thing, Hunt—given your history—letting you be there."

"And what's my history?" Hunt said. "What are you referring to?"

"Your history is *visions*," Leah said. "Your history is the inside of your head...and not being able to make critical distinctions, sometimes, between it and the outside world."

"I see," Hunt said.

"Yes, I know," Leah said. "You see and see and see...and that's, occasionally, a problem. A very serious problem. And of course I *don't* see. And that's *my* problem. Because when I don't see—I feel backed up and I strike out. I shoot whatever off—verbal mace—into the darkness where I can only sense I-don't-know-what shapes moving."

Hunt and Leah both broke down over the phone and asked for each other's patience and each other's forgiveness. Hunt said he didn't think it would be much longer. "Oh, did you hear about the cocaine baker?" he asked.

"The what? Excuse me, Hunt, did you say the *cocaine baker*?"

"Never mind. I'm sorry. Let it go," Hunt said, although he felt a strange kind of personal grief about the incident and about the man. Then he said again: "I suspect...my sense is that it really isn't going to be much longer."

Leah just laughed.

• • •

And it wasn't. Much longer. At about 2 a.m. on the fourth day, Melissa Probert struggled awake. It was as though her body were reclaiming life one cell at a time, each cell stopping to consider its individual choice. Hunt shot picture after picture for an hour and a half. He slapped new roll after new roll into the cameras. "What you are taking," Melissa said, "what you are photographing is dead matter reconstituting *mind*. And although it *looks* like it's taking only hours the fact is that's an illusion because it's all... it's all *time lapse*: it's the trick of time lapse. The *actual* coming to life has taken nearly 70 billion years."

Melissa's eyes were fixed and full, her body poised and steady. There seemed an almost terrible resolve in her.

She said nothing more. She stood. Hunt kept taking pictures. She studied the space, her home. She walked over to where the fuchsia had gone through the large-paned window, reached out a finger, and perilously touched a jagged edge of glass. She walked over to the exploded television set. She kicked the various thirty-gallon garbage bags Hunt had filled, kicked them the way someone considering a used car kicks a tire. "A mess!" was all she finally said. "A mess! I was a mess, wasn't I? I was wasted protein."

"Well..."

"*Say* it."

"To a major extent," Hunt said.

"To a major extent," Melissa Probert repeated. "To a major extent. Wasted. Yes, I'm sure."

"Should I keep taking?" Hunt asked.

Melissa shook her head. "No, we're through," she said. "We're through; it's done—or, hopefully, *begun*—. At any rate, we're finished." She crossed into the kitchen. "Well, you've certainly been being a good boy all the while. I can see that. Fresh coffee. Papers all lined up, Tuesday through Friday. How many times have you had to clean the house?"

"It doesn't matter," Hunt said.

"You left the window for me to see, though, didn't you?" Melissa said.

"Yes, I did," Hunt confessed.

"And the television."

"And the television. That's accurate; that's true."

"You're a good friend," Melissa said. And she walked to Hunt, hugged him, and began to cry. She cried for nearly half an hour. She had no words, or if she did she didn't speak them. Hunt led her to the couch and held her there like a child. It was nearly 4. When she was finished crying, she said two things. She said: "I suspect—or maybe the right verb is *pray*—I *pray* I will never drink again," and she said: "How about some breakfast? I'll cook."

Hunt said breakfast would be a treat.

• • •

Melissa made huevos rancheros. "It's a test," she said. "If I can face huevos rancheros, I can face the most ravaged and mangled parts of myself."

It seemed to Hunt she meant it.

Melissa put on a CD of Purcell. She hummed with the trumpets as she stirred the eggs. Hunt watched and listened. "Hunt, have a drink for me," she said over her shoulder. "Then have another and another. I'm just kidding." She started crying again, and Hunt moved up behind her and rubbed her back.

Eating, she took each bite slowly, savoring it with what appeared to be relief. She held each taste of coffee in her mouth. "I feel like good sex," she said finally. "I really do. I feel like I want some good sex."

Hunt fantasized an image of Leah at the kitchen window: white-faced, peering in. He smiled, said nothing, nodded.

"Do you feel like some good sex?" Melissa asked.

"I'll have another piece of chorizo," Hunt said.

"You didn't answer my question."

"Uh…sure," Hunt said. He smiled.

"With me?"

"Um…no," Hunt said.

"No?!" Melissa acted mock-outraged. "No?! With *who* then? *Whom*."

"I don't…I don't know," Hunt said. He felt relieved, curiously rested.

"You feel like good sex, but you don't know who with?!" Melissa Probert repeated.

Hunt laughed. "Look, I'm sorry," he said. He hoped the mock interrogation would end.

"*Sorry* isn't the word!" Melissa said. She laughed. "*Sorry* doesn't *begin* to tell the story. I'm serious: who with? With the Virgin Mary? You have someone else? Woman in your life you're not talking about?

Secret friend? New face? Listen, level with me! Who with?! With the baker who died? With a candle flame?"

Hunt shrugged.

"Hunt..." She had him going and knew it. They were both enjoying the lift and freedom. "Hunt, do you know the difference between us?" Melissa asked.

"No, Melissa," Hunt said; "no, I don't. So tell me. Enlighten me. Lead me to the truth. What *is* the difference between us?"

"The difference between us," Melissa said, "is that I insult *myself*, while you let *others* insult *you*. And that's why I'm a photojournalist and you paint."

"Well, I've never thought of that," Hunt confessed. "I've never thought of it quite—I don't think—that way."

They kissed good-bye. Dawn was approaching. Hunt drove home, his favorite country and western station playing all the sleepy and dreamy Willie Nelson and Crystal Gayle that the morning could manage. Both Hunt's windows were down. His eyes were pooled with tears at the edges—as sometimes happened when gratitude rushed too suddenly through him, its reasons still outside his reach. His heart felt contained and palpable. He tasted sweetness on his lips—then he realized it wasn't just there on his lips; it was outside, in the air, as well.

In his headlights the route looked glazed, looked buttered. Hunt realized where he was. He was at the site—or fast approaching it—where the baker had met the pole. And then he saw. He pulled over and got out of the car. He had to know. In the days since, in the intervening days, someone had constructed a shrine. There was a post. And on the post—of shaped and painted ceramic—was a loaf of bread. And within the loaf burned a candle. *Oh, Christ!* Hunt thought. *Christ!*

He knelt. Bowed his head. His life came up and then out in tears. Because he saw his son Sean in the flame, the shrine. It was still dark. It was still dark enough for there to be all that ache and mystery.

• • •

That night Leah said, "You have to understand: what you do with your life—the seeing, the way it all shifts and changes—I don't want it. I don't want it in *my* life—from now on, I guess is what I'm saying,

Hunt. I'd rather it weren't like this. Because sometimes it leaves me very alone. And I'm saying, sometimes it frightens me."

Hunt put an arm around her, tried to think of a reply. None came. None sufficient, really, to match her candor. Only faint aureoles of light—not his, the night's—which played always in the far corners.

The Fish Magician

1

Malcolm hears the call, the invitation, and rises from his seat, his wife Ginger's hand like a heat phantom floating in the air behind him—pushing him forward? staying him? It's hard to tell. Malcolm climbs the stairs, mounts the stage, says hello to the thin magician, shakes his hand, steps into a box windowed by Lucite, pinned by light. And—seeing the man with the cape furl something huge and purple, something velveteen, up and into the air over the box (if there is sound, it is sound hushed), then seeing no more, seeing nothing because seeing leaps beyond vision, becomes gem colored before anything's seen, some essential ardor of emerald, ruby, some hard-colored truth in a gale wind that sucks every bone into his breath. Malcolm feels himself hurled—somewhere north, off the stage, out of the theater, casino, resort: out of town, finally, across one state line, possibly two, where it smells like juniper, a thousand edgeless rocks, heron feathers. One can imagine Idaho. Why not? A sign, print burned into wood then stained, says Magic Reservoir. Why not. Malcolm listens for clues and hears only a world beyond traffic.

2

All I ever wanted to be was funny. But fate deals the cards. They call sports the gateway into whatever you'd do if you had brains or talent. I was a second-string All American, playing four years with the Cincinnati Bengals, four more with the San Diego Chargers. Truth's funny when you say it right. And we get second chances. So, funny was what I tried to be, broadcasting *Monday Night Football* with the Wildebeest and the Prince of Nose Candy, but the network saw what I thought hilarious differently, told me shut up or leave. Be reasonable. How does a broadcaster shut up? So I left, made a little noise, went on talk shows for a year—did you know Boomer Esiason?—never mind—got sued twice, run down by a car (not an accident), body knocked into a ditch in a remote Saskatchewan (I think the word is) village. For a week I was the missing body. But then I regained what I've realized, since then, is more than consciousness, found myself, climbed up onto the road, got found, came here, and now do what I do: try to employ my more-than-consciousness, find other people, audition, do the comedy clubs.

True story: I'm taking lunch at the Mirage California Pizza Kitchen so I can watch the sportsbook with a pair of hundred-power Bushnells, and this woman comes up—handsome, mid-forties, jewelry, nicely accessorized—asks am I who I am? Is my casebook full? Good, because she has a missing body.

The missing body's her husband. They went to see Lance Burton at the Monte Carlo last night. *Great show!* she said, *great show! Have you seen it?* Of course. *Somewhere around*—she looked at her watch—*10:46, Lance asks for someone in the audience.* Woman's husband's a magic freak, been one since he was a kid, pops up out of his seat, goes up, steps into the box; Lance makes him disappear, does seven other tricks, levitates himself on a motorcycle, road-trips the air—blue smoke.

The show ends, the theater empties. My lady's waiting, waiting. She's the only one in the theater except a stagehand; he says, *Ma'am?* She says, *Lance Burton made my husband—my husband Malcolm—disappear. Where would he—?* Stagehand has no idea. *Wait here*, he says. It's five, ten, fifteen minutes. Man comes out in a suit, looking very casino: *Would you come with me?* he asks. My lady follows; the two go into an office. Clearly executive, clearly management: office is like a suite, full bar, entertainment center. *What would you like to drink?* the executive asks. *Any piroshki? Dolmathes?* She repeats her story: *Where's my husband?*

Sit down, the executive suit says. *Please. I need to explain something.* But first he makes her sign a paper saying all he tells her will be in strictest confidence.

She does. As much of a suit as the executive is, the guy is shaking; he's a man probably plays golf six out of seven and he's white. *Something tragic is happening*, he says. Lance Burton—one of the great magicians of the world, the man for whom the Monte Carlo built and designed their present show room—is losing his memory. *Hands are fine*, executive says. *Skill's as nimble as ever. The man defines 'dexterous.' Short-term, though, is another matter.*

Where's my husband? my lady asks.

We wish we knew, executive says. He'd asked Lance. *Lance, you remember making the gentleman in the black turtleneck, brown houndstooth disappear?*

Lance said yes.

So, do you remember where you disappeared him to?

Lance said no.

Trust me: Lance feels terrible. He feels humiliated. He knows what is happening to him. And I have to tell you, it's unforgiving. It's cruel. One of the great magicians of the world.

Where does Lance disappear most of his things, most of the people?

Different places.

Like?

Apparently, there's no pattern. That was part of Lance's fun. Sometimes the ballroom of the MGM. *The further away, the more the challenge*, is what Lance had said. And in the last year—almost to defy loss of memory—he'd pushed. One time he'd made a horse disappear and the horse showed up onstage with Rosie O'Donnell in Atlantic City.

My lady had asked around, and I had a certain reputation—or infamy—for finding missing bodies. She'd read a hack piece in *Sports Illustrated* about the network firing me and how that had led to me finding missing bodies. The Monte Carlo would pay. Would I talk to Lance? Would I take the case?

One of the funniest books in the Old Testament, I think, is Job. His boils kill me. It cracks me up how Job says, *Let the night be solitary*. How do you come up with a line like that? Job's like Chaplin, he's like this ancient little tramp who can't get anything; it's a riot. Chapter 10 is comic genius. Verse 10: *Hast thou not poured me out as milk, curdled me like cheese?* I mean, it's just one of those things that's funny—same way Wisconsin is funny. Except I would have ended Job differently. Cut chapter 42, had it end where the darts are counted as stubble and he's laughing at a shaking spear. I'm working up a whole Job routine, and I wouldn't mind being a warm-up at the Monte Carlo.

So I say yes. *Have the Monte Carlo call Lance. Also, have them agree: the missing body in return for one night in Lance's Evening of Magic.*

Do you have an intuition? my lady asks.

I see fields of mission bells, bitterroot. *Idaho*, I say.

Idaho? she puzzles. *But there's no connection. We have no connection whatsoever with Idaho; we've never been there.*

All the more reason for the intuition, I say.

Lance is at a loss when I take him through guided imagery over the phone. His voice sags on all the unaccented syllables. He tries. Still, he comes up with postcards: lava rock, watercress, a blue heron. *I'm missing a dove*, he tells me, *a small water fountain . . . half an assistant.*

I'll keep my eyes out, I tell him. A dove, a small fountain, half an assistant—lava rock, watercress, a blue heron. I take the elevator to the top of the Stratosphere, walk around and around the windblown observation deck. I call my lady, whose name is Ginger. *Any word?* I ask. Before Ginger can answer, a second cell I'd forgotten I had in my pocket rings, Ginger hears it, says, *Any chance it's Malcolm?* But it's the Monte Carlo, asking if she's still in town, but I don't tell her that.

I take a cab up the Boulevard, walk around backstage, am let into the Magic Room, touch boxes, blades of swords, birdcages. *Idaho!* everything whispers—like sex, like the relics of saints—*Idaho!* There are three blood-carpeted stairs to a small platform; I climb them. I disappear, just for a moment, then reappear. My breathing's shallow, rock-washed, filled with ozone. I leave the Magic Room, call Ginger. *Meet me at Sfuzzi's*, I say, 7:00, *in the Fashion Mall. It's across from the Dive.*

I root out Ginger's executive—a man with sunken eyes, sunken cheeks, and a nose that's listing. I say, *Mr. Castelli, I need an hour with Lance.*

Castelli's voice wants to scramble my signal. He's all distrust pretending to be cooperation. He says, *I guess, okay, if a lawyer's present. But don't get any ideas; you're going to have to prove magical negligence.*

Lance Burton's by his pool, with a lawyer. The air's sheeted like phyllo; light's like lava rock. *Make something disappear,* I say. I'm just trying to find a handle. *It doesn't have to be difficult; anything.*

He chooses the water in the pool. It's gone; the pool's dry, then it's back again.

Interesting, I say. *Do it again. Something else.* He's wearing a bathing suit with pictures of fish. The fish disappear; it's a solid blue suit, then the rainbows are back again. *One more time,* I request. He's eating a salad. He waves his hand, and that's the end of the watercress; it's just radicchio. *You're good,* I say. That's the word on the street and I can't dispute it. *Bring the watercress back.*

Bring the what back? Lance Burton says, and the lawyer whispers something into his ear.

We do word association and it might as well be sand blasting. I say *coriander*; he says *sigmoidoscopy.* I ask has he ever seen Malcolm before last night—in videotape, perhaps, or a photograph? Any prior conversations with Malcolm's Ginger?

The Monte Carlo lawyer leans in, whispers. *We take exception to your implications,* he says. *Mr. Burton's no hit magician.*

Except he is a hit magician, I say, and though it's reasonably quick, it's not funny.

I meet Ginger at Sfuzzi's. When the hostess asks inside or outside, I say, *It's the story of my life.*

Ginger prefers inside—where she feels more volume, she says, more shape. They have conditioner ducts the color of jicama. We split an insalata mista and I order a bottle of Marilyn Merlot—you take your laughs wherever.

What've you found? Ginger asks, and on this particular night—full moon, Strip traffic like gelatin, the sound of the Dive next door hitting the bottom of the ocean—*What've you found?* seems such a delicious question.

I have a theory about inevitability. Greek tragedy used to be comedy before it was tragedy. The House of Atreus was originally a funhouse—something happened to the mirrors; Sophocles broke one, then figured *fuck it,* broke them all. Discoveries used to be marriages before they were blindings; people spilled wine, not blood; professional football used to be professional magic before special teams. It's the mirror thing all over—again and again. Back at the beginning, fish had feathers.

Ginger had merlot on her upper lip, the unwashed crust of a crying jag on one cheekbone. Bodies get lost—isn't that amazing?—but not forever. That you can find the missing body again and again is, I think, a miracle. What had I found out?

It's indisputable, I say.

What's indisputable?

Idaho.

Idaho's indisputable?

Absolutely.

How can Idaho be indisputable?

You're wild, Ginger.

Seriously.

Because, look at us. Look at where we are.

Yes, she says.

Smell the night, I say.

She does.

I say, *Idaho's the next state.*

3

Malcolm supports himself against a lodgepole at the foot of the spillway. *I was somewhere*, he thinks. *Somewhere in a world not here—where was that?* Folded on the stones are his black turtleneck, brown houndstooth. There are plovers, Steller's jays on branches. Indigo buntings browse the ground thatch: seeds? With each inquiry of beak: seeds? Seeds? The water falling sounds like applause.

Where had he been? Memory, in this place, seems very much like a binnacle in a kitchen in Oklahoma—a thing unnecessary. Malcolm thinks of *the inevitability of water!* Of the *comedy of light!* He forgoes connections—because there are open birdcages in a logjam of tamarack and black hawthorn, nesting cinnamon teal, rock dove. There's a small fountain lodged in a listing Engelmann. Colored scarves blow by like sheeting rain. In a field rife with Russian thistle, beyond which horses dance, is half a woman. Upper.

Oh, my dear! Malcolm says.

Hello! the half woman says. *Take a card—any card! My name's Sheila!*

What happened? Malcolm says.

Isn't this all wonderful? Sheila says. *Finally? At last?*

But you're only half here, Malcolm says.

At least I'm half here, Sheila says. Then, *Look! Oh, look!* She points to a purple cape floating by on the Big Wood River.

Two others, a man and a woman, climb the horizon of barbed wire, up over what seems a stairway and down: the man lank and overburdened with sinew, the woman's wrists mirrors of atmosphere. Between them, a picnic basket and a boom box. The boom box plays Kenny G.

Ginger! Malcolm says.

Idaho! Ginger says.

The lank man, wishing he could be funny, points behind to a small ladder he and his companion had climbed.

Sportsman's access, he says. *It says Magic Reservoir sportsman's access.*

About the Author

David Kranes is the author of eight novels and three volumes of short stories, including *Low Tide in the Desert*, *Keno Runner: A Dark Romance*, and *Abracadabra*, all published by the University of Nevada Press. He is professor emeritus of English at the University of Utah and lives in Salt Lake City.